SHOWDOWN AT SINGING SPRINGS

Deputy Sheriff Chuck Kendrick had a burning desire to meet up with the notorious Darra gang, his father's vicious killers. But fate seemed to conspire against him — until Sheriff Lorimer set him to watching Al Ensor, an itinerant pedlar. The towns Ensor visited seemed to get robbed by the Darra gang, so Kendrick rode out, and immediately found himself knee-deep in trouble. He came up against overwhelming odds, but still had to face the greatest challenge of all — the showdown at Singing Springs.

Books by Corba Sunman
in the Linford Western Library:

RANGE WOLVES
LONE HAND
GUN TALK
TRIGGER LAW
GUNSMOKE JUSTICE
BIG TROUBLE
GUN PERIL

CORBA SUNMAN

SHOWDOWN AT SINGING SPRINGS

Complete and Unabridged

LINFORD
Leicester

First published in Great Britain in 2003 by
Robert Hale Limited
London

First Linford Edition
published 2005
by arrangement with
Robert Hale Limited
London

British Library CIP Data

Sunman, Corba
    Showdown at singing springs.—Large print ed.—
Linford western library
    1. Western stories
    2. Large type books
    I. Title
    823.9'14 [F]

    ISBN 1–84395–609–8

Published by
F. A. Thorpe (Publishing)
Anstey, Leicestershire

Set by Words & Graphics Ltd.
Anstey, Leicestershire
Printed and bound in Great Britain by
T. J. International Ltd., Padstow, Cornwall

This book is printed on acid-free paper

1

Sheriff's Deputy Chuck Kendrick first saw smoke from a distance, rising on the breeze like an Indian beacon. But he knew it could not be the work of redskins, and spurred his black into a run across the short grass plain towards the ominous smudge. There had been two ranch fires in Bender County in the past month, and neither of them could be attributed to careless ranchers. The overhead sun glinted on the law star pinned on Kendrick's shirt, and after two years in the job he was beginning to wish he had not taken the oath to uphold the laws of the State of Texas. Lawlessness was rife in the county, murder commonplace, and those unknowns responsible for the crime wave were not over-endowed with conscience.

At twenty-four, Kendrick was three

inches over six feet and weighed 200 pounds of muscle and sinew — the first ten years of his working life as a cowboy on the western side of the Blue Hills had kept him at the peak of physical fitness. But a bad fall from a horse had broken his left leg, which, badly set at the time, left him with a pronounced limp and ended his career as a cowhand.

He topped a rise and reined in to gaze across the intervening ground at the distant Bar S ranch, where the crazy column of smoke was billowing into the sky. The ominous red glow of a fire that had taken serious hold indicated that the ranch house was beyond saving, and he pushed the black into a run down the slope and on to the blazing building. A bucket chain had been formed by the crew, but was obviously having little effect.

Ben Slater, the Bar S rancher, stepped out of the line of sweating punchers when he heard Kendrick's approach. Tall, thin, and looking every day of his sixty years, Slater's blue eyes were ablaze with anger and shock. He turned and glanced at his burning headquarters, shook his head sadly, and dropped a hand to the butt of the .45 Colt holstered on his right hip. He grasped Kendrick's reins as the deputy pulled his horse to a slithering halt and dismounted fast.

'Hell, Chuck, am I glad to see you! But it's a pity you didn't show up half an hour ago. There was a bunch of riders here — mebbe six — who killed Pete Webb and Mike Doan before firing the house and splitting the breeze. We were out on the range when we saw smoke, and came back to find the fire had too strong a hold to be put out.'

Kendrick spotted the bodies of the two dead punchers lying on the ground by the well and a pang of horror struck through him. He shook his head. He and Pete Webb had been friends for a long time.

'Did you get a good look at the riders?' he grated, choking back his shock.

'They had left the yard when we showed up. It looked like they was heading to town. We had a choice of taking out after them or trying to save the house. Heck, you must have passed those galoots on your way in.'

Kendrick shook his head. 'Nope. I was at Circle B before coming on here. Frank Belmont rode into town last evening to see the sheriff. He's lost more than a hundred head of cattle. A bunch of wideloopers ran 'em off into the canyon country — making for the Mex border, I guess.'

'Have you or the sheriff any idea what's going on? The county has always been kind of lawless, being close to the border, but it was never this bad, not even in the old days.' Slater gazed at the raging fire, bitterness etched on his weathered face. 'Thirty years I've been here,' he grated, 'and I've never known anything but trouble. But the Injuns couldn't run me out, and I'll be damned if wideloopers will. Are you heading back to town?'

4

'Yeah. Abe told me to head right back after checking with Belmont. But I had the ride for nothing. Circle B are out tracking the rustlers.'

'That's what I would expect. But we both know Frank will be wasting his time. Those badhats are too well organized around here. With all this trouble spreading, the law department should take on more deputies. Tell Lorimer I'll be in to see him sometime soon.'

Kendrick nodded, his eyes on Pete Webb, and there was a sickness deep inside him — the same feeling he had experienced when, at the age of twelve, they had told him his father, the town marshal in Bleak Ridge to the west of the county, had been killed trying to foil a bank raid. 'Is there anything I can do before I ride on, Ben?' he asked.

Slater shook his head. 'God Almighty couldn't help me now! I'm gonna take out after the buzzards who did this, and I won't give in until the last one of them is buried. If the law can't help us then we've got to do the dirty work ourselves.' He shrugged resignedly and bitterness crept into his tone. 'Hell, we've done it before so it'll be nothing new.'

Kendrick looked at the doomed ranch house. The roof was a mass of roaring flames, the heat terrific. The cowboys were giving up their task, and came to surround Kendrick and their boss. Big Jake Sarn, the Bar S foreman, wiped sweat from his forehead. His face was showing conflicting emotions. Tall and big-boned, he looked like a small giant, dwarfing even Kendrick. His eyes were startlingly blue, his hair yellow like ripe corn, and when he spoke his voice did not betray even a fraction of his Scandinavian ancestry.

'We're wasting time, boss,' he said. 'We oughta be chasing those hardcases.'

'I guess you're right, Jake.' Slater drew his pistol and examined its loads. He looked into Kendrick's eyes. 'We'll be seeing you in town later, Chuck, and you can tell Abe that we won't be put

6

off again. He's had too many chances to set things right, and we've been fools to listen to him.' He lifted his gun and waved it. 'This is the only law in Bender County right now, and we're sure as hell gonna use it.'

'Don't go off half-cocked, Ben,' Kendrick warned.

Slater uttered an exclamation of impatience and turned away. His crew departed for their horses waiting in the nearby corral, and Kendrick stood watching until the grim-faced punchers were riding out of the yard. He looked once more at the raging fire, and his gaze encompassed the inert body of his dead friend. He shook his head and swung into his saddle, grimacing as his left leg protested at the movement. He leaned his weight to the right in the saddle, waiting for the darting shafts of agony to subside, then touched spurs to the black's flanks and turned the animal to head for Clearwater Creek.

For a couple of miles he rode, eating the dust raised by the Bar S outfit, his eyes busy watching the tracks that the cowpunchers were following. At one point he dismounted and dropped to one knee to examine the tracks closely, satisfying himself that he would recognize some of the hoofprints again. He continued to town. His thoughts were dark and brooding. He knew that bad trouble was coming to this range, and he was caught up in the middle of it.

He was aware that these days Abe Lorimer was not the best sheriff in the world. Lorimer had run the county law department since before Kendrick had been born. He had fought Indians and Mexicans in the old days. But at sixty-two his heyday was long past, and it seemed to Kendrick, having had the opportunity to view the sheriff closely, that the man was too old to hold down what had become a monstrous chore. Only his reputation stilled the tongues of those men in the county who wanted change, but even Lorimer's staunchest supporters were becoming disillusioned by the law department's failure to stem the rising tide of lawlessness.

When Clearwater Creek came into sight, Kendrick gazed dispassionately at the single street. The buildings on either side were mainly of adobe, unlovely in the strong sunlight, looking dingy and uncared for. There were no sidewalks, wood being scarce in this region, and the general view of the place was such that Kendrick could not tell by merely looking if he were in Mexico or not.

His gaze roved along the length of the street and his expression hardened when he saw Sheriff Lorimer seated as usual on his favourite chair situated on the right side of the jail doorway, watching the small world of Clearwater Creek passing by, ready to swap pleasantries or the time of day with those inclined to discourse with him.

Kendrick grimaced, his mind still occupied with the mental image of Pete Webb and Mike Doan lying stretched out dead in the yard of Bar S. He rode along the street and reined up in front of the law office, aware that he was suddenly reluctant to face his boss. Abe Lorimer was small and wiry, his face the colour of old leather. His big white Stetson was pulled forward over his bird-like eyes and he was wearing his faithful twin .44 Colt pistols that somehow had always seemed too large for his small hands. Lounging on his chair and gazing impassively at Kendrick, he waited for a report. Completely at ease, he looked as if his bailiwick was the most lawful in the entire state.

Kendrick made his report in a flat tone, his mind occupied by a mental image of the two dead cowboys lying out at Bar S, and he was aware that somehow his whole attitude to law-dealing had changed subtly during his ride back to town. He watched Lorimer sigh and close his eyes as if he had dropped off to sleep, and waited, his voice trailing off. He was accustomed to the diminutive sheriff's mannerisms. Lorimer's blue eyes suddenly popped open and regarded Kendrick's big figure.

'So what do you reckon we should do, Chuck?' Lorimer scratched his close-shaven chin and pushed back his white Stetson to wipe beads of sweat from his rugged forehead. 'It sure is hot today,' he complained. 'Sixty years in this country and I still ain't used to the weather! So things are popping out there on the range, huh? I guessed they would. That's why I sent Bill Watt out patrolling through Blanco Canyon to look for rustled stock being moved to the border. With any luck he should spot those stolen Circle B steers and get a good look at the rustlers. And Bar S has gone up in smoke! The hell you say! Heck, I'll betcha Ben Slater is madder than a wet hen. I sure hope he catches up with the buzzards responsible. If he does get a line on who did it, you deputies can ride out and arrest them.'

Kendrick shook his head as he considered. He could imagine the hot iron that Lorimer had been, for the sheriff used to be hell on wheels in Bender County before age took the edge off his ability. Now the sheriff was content to bask in faded glory, content to delegate law-dealing to his deputies; a mere pale replica of his former self, and it was a wonder that the electorate who kept him in office could still indulge him, considering all the trouble that was breaking out.

'What do you want me to do now, Abe?' Kendrick fought down an impulse to quit the job cold. The sight of Pete Webb lying dead had disillusioned him, and it had taken the ride back to town to crystallize his feelings to the point of wanting out of the restrictions that Lorimer imposed on his deputies.

'You've been in the saddle a good few hours, Chuck, and your horse looks jaded. Always keep your horse in a good state of readiness, son. You'll never know when you might need it, and a tired horse won't get you far once you leave town limits.'

'When was the last time you rode out of town?' Kendrick enquired.

Lorimer eyed him suspiciously, then

decided he was not being sarcastic and grinned.

'I got better things to do these days than ride the range like an idiot, trying the old-fashioned ways of detecting crime. I'm better occupied directing you younger men to the spots where you're most needed.'

'Mebbe that's why we're getting so much trouble, Abe. You can't get around like you did in the old days. The badmen have got the upper hand and you ain't able to stop them.'

Lorimer's gaunt face changed expression as he took in Kendrick's words. He stiffened in his seat and his eyes narrowed.

'Well now,' he said softly. 'You've been one of my deputies now for mebbe two years, so you figure you've got enough experience to teach an old dog like me some newfangled tricks of handling the law, huh? You reckon, because you've probably got the fastest gun in Texas, that your speed makes you tops in everything else. Well, pin back your ears and listen good, Chuck. You ain't begun to learn anything yet. Ten years in the job just mebbe give you some idea of what's what.'

'I reckon I know enough to decide that I ain't cut out to be an errand boy for you, running around in circles like a chicken with its head cut off while you sit here every day like your britches are stuck to the seat. I reckon I should be working on my own, watching points and working out what steps I oughta take. To my way of thinking, the law has got to be tougher than the owlhoots, and we ain't that — no sir — not by a long rope.'

'So give me the benefit of your wisdom and experience and tell me how you would handle this here situation?' Lorimer grinned smugly and waited, and when Kendrick shrugged, the sheriff stood up, the top of his head barely reaching up to his deputy's wide shoulders. He had to step backwards in order to look into Kendrick's troubled brown eyes, then

14

nodded. 'Yeah, Chuck, I can see what your trouble is. You been hit bad by Pete Webb's death. Take a coupla days off duty and relax. Forget about the law. You're sweet on Sammy Jo Ives, so I've heard tell, so why don't you ride out to Triangle I and spend some time with that gal? You'll soon come back to yourself, I promise you. Then you'll be ready to return and get on with what you do best.'

'I don't need a vacation.' Kendrick shook his head impatiently. 'If you gave me my head, Sheriff, I reckon I'd break the back of this trouble inside of a week. For a start I'd clean out some of the snakes in this town who are hiding their true faces behind respectable jobs.'

'Now steady up, son. You sound like you're keen to go off half-cocked, and that ain't good. My advice is sound. You take off to Triangle I for at least a week. That's an order, you hear? I don't wanta notice your face around town again until I've seen out next Sunday.

You got that straight?'

Kendrick shook his head, fighting a wave of black emotion that threatened to overwhelm him. Ever since his father was killed he had been fighting a battle against his darker inclinations.

'I don't go along with that at all, Abe,' he said doggedly. 'The way I'm feeling right now, I'd be better off quitting. This ain't the kind of law-dealing I hanker for.'

'It sounds to me now like your father is talking,' Lorimer said. 'And he's been dead these past twelve years, to my reckoning. Mind you, I never knew a better lawman. He had it all. But if there was anything wrong with his work it was a little streak of recklessness that crept into him at times. He never should have gone for those bank robbers bald-headed. If he had fetched help instead of taking on those smokeroos alone, he'd be alive today. No, son. Don't quit cold. Go away and think it over for a spell. Keep your badge on, come back later, and I promise that you'll feel a whole heap better when you do.'

Kendrick turned away without further comment and took up his reins. He led the black along the street to the livery barn, feeling completely out of sorts. He felt as if his mind was carrying an intolerable burden and there was no way he could shed the load. Leading the black to the water trough outside the stable, he permitted it to drink roughly half its fill, then led it into the barn and put it in a stall. There was no sign of Tom Ford, the liveryman, so he went to the big barrel just inside the doorway and helped himself to a scoop of milled grain which he put into the black's manger.

It was then that he heard voices raised in sudden altercation — one a woman's — coming from a stall towards the rear of the barn, and the raw fear lacing the female's tone was enough to send Kendrick limping to investigate. His right hand dropped to the butt of his holstered gun and from force of habit he eased it as he moved forward silently.

The voices cut off as suddenly as they had started. Kendrick peered into the last stall on the left and saw a girl he did not know standing with her back to a small white cow pony. She was cowering from a big man who was confronting her with a long-bladed hunting-knife in his right hand. The man's back was towards Kendrick.

'What's going on here?' Kendrick demanded.

The man whirled surprisingly fast and lunged at Kendrick without hesitation, the point of his knife spearing forward to stab. Kendrick took a half-step backwards, swaying his upper body to his right, and the knife-point missed him by a hair's-breadth. His big left fist, clenched into a club, swung in a furious arc and connected with a meaty smack against a stubbled jaw. The man went over backwards like a tree falling in a hurricane and landed at the girl's feet, unconscious.

Kendrick limped forward, bent and picked up the discarded knife, which was glinting in the straw, and removed a pistol from the man's holster. He straightened and looked at the girl. She was dressed in dun-coloured female range clothes; a neat little vest that was close-fitting, and tight pants that hugged her lithe figure like a second skin. Her tanned face was pale with shock, her blue eyes wide with fright. Although he reckoned she was about twenty years old, she gazed at him like a child who had awakened in the middle of a nightmare.

She moistened her lips as if to speak, but the big man on the ground began to stir, and Kendrick checked the gun he had taken and then cocked it, covering the groaning figure.

'So tell me what this is all about,' Kendrick said, eyeing the girl for she was good to look at. 'You're a stranger in town, and so's he.' He stirred the man with the toe of his boot. 'Come on, mister, wake up. You're making the stable look untidy. If you wanta sleep, I know just the place where you can do it.'

'Please,' the girl said. 'Don't make anything of this. It's not what it seems. He's tracked me into town and wants to take me back to my father. I was refusing to go when you stepped in.'

'He was trying to persuade you with a knife?' Kendrick frowned. 'That's against the law for a start. And he attempted to stick me with it, which is another offence. Give me some answers to the questions going round in my head. Who are you and where'd you come from. And who's this big lug when he's on his feet? If he ain't seen the inside of a jail before today then I miss my guess. He's sure making this place look untidy, and a spell in jail just might make him better mannered.'

'I'm Jenny Ensor. My father is Al Ensor, a travelling salesman. We're camped by a creek to the south a few miles out of town. Pa was planning on coming in tomorrow to sell his wares, but I couldn't wait to shake the dust of the wilderness off my feet, and I guess Pa sent Buster to fetch me back to camp.'

Kendrick frowned. 'Is your father a medicine man? I heard tell there was one through here last year, and when he left, half the folks in town turned mighty sick.'

'Oh no!' she protested. 'Pa travels in household goods — pots, pans, everything for the home. He has a good reputation for his wares.'

Kendrick nodded. 'So this is Buster, huh?' He covered the fallen man, who was beginning to take an interest in his surroundings. 'Buster who?'

'Buster Fenton. He works with my father. I'm sorry Buster got off on the wrong foot with you.'

'Wrong foot! Heck, he nearly got me with his pig-sticker. That ain't no way for an honest man to act. I'll take him to see the sheriff, and you better come along. There's too much violence in these parts without strangers showing up and adding to it. And don't go

21

giving me no arguments,' he added as she opened her mouth to speak.

He turned to bend over Fenton, and as he grasped the man to haul him upright it seemed that the roof of the stable fell in on him. A black curtain dropped before his eyes and he fell to the ground, unaware that the girl had pulled a rifle from the saddle boot on her horse and slammed the butt against his head.

2

When he regained his senses, Kendrick opened his eyes to find himself gazing up into the bearded face of Tom Ford, the frail old liveryman, whose gaunt face was showing amazement as he gazed at the fallen deputy. Kendrick pushed himself into a sitting position and raised a hand to his aching head. He found a lump the size of a hen's egg on the back of his skull, and his fingers came away smeared with blood. Grabbing at his Stetson, which had fallen from his head, he lurched to his feet, gritting his teeth as undue pressure sent a shaft of pain through his badly set leg.

'Did you see a man and a woman in here, Tom?' he asked, reaching for a rail and hanging on to it. 'The girl had a horse in this stall, a little white cow pony.'

'I saw them riding out,' Ford replied.

'I was heading back along the street when they came out of the barn almost at a gallop. They sure were in a hurry! I thought the place was on fire. But now I know what was pushing them. What for did they hit you?'

'It was the woman. I thought I was saving her from the man, but she hit me from behind. Which way did they ride?'

'North. But I wouldn't set no store by that. They might circle round once clear of town and head south.'

Kendrick grimaced. 'Well, that figures. She did tell me they were camped at the little creek south of town. Did you see her earlier, when she brought her horse in?'

'Nope. They must have come in after I left. I've been in the store at least an hour. They sure didn't stay long, huh? Must have been up to no good when you disturbed them.'

'That's what I figure.' Kendrick eased his hat on to his head and went back to his horse. He tightened the girth and led the animal out of the barn.

Swinging into the saddle, he touched spurs to the animal's flanks and headed north, riding along the street at a fast clip. When he passed the law office he lifted a hand to the lounging sheriff, and kept on riding when Lorimer called to him. He left town, squinting his eyes against the glare of the sun. His head ached, and he was furiously determined to catch his assailants.

He spotted two sets of fresh tracks and followed them, nodding to himself when they suddenly veered away to the right and swung in a wide arc until they were heading south. He bypassed the town, hit open range, and spotted a banner of dust rising in the air ahead which marked the progress of the two riders he was pursuing. Nodding to himself, he eased away to the right, not wanting them to spot him. If the girl had told the truth about where they were camping then he knew their destination. As he rode, he wondered why they were being so devious, and concluded that they were up to no good.

He put a ridge between himself and his quarry and rode fast, making for the small creek the girl had mentioned. When he reached it he reined in behind a crest, left his horse with trailing reins, and dismounted to walk forward slowly until he could peer over the skyline. He saw a small Conestoga wagon parked beside the creek, canvas top and all. Two horses were grazing by the creek, knee-hobbled so they could not stray, and there was an oldish man tending a small fire downwind of the wagon. Kendrick went back to his black, climbed into the saddle and rode over to the creek.

The man in the camp was middle-aged, probably in his early fifties. He turned from the fire when he heard Kendrick splashing through the creek, and made a fast grab for the pistol in the holster on his right hip, but stayed his hand when Kendrick's gun came into play to cover him. He shrugged and thrust his weapon deep into its holster. Tall and thin, he looked sickly, and held his hands well clear of his cadaverous body.

'Howdy,' he greeted. 'You kinda took me by surprise, coming in like that. A man is apt to collect a chunk of lead, sneaking around a camp.'

'I wasn't sneaking,' Kendrick replied sourly. 'You're Al Ensor, huh?'

'Sure. But I don't reckon we've met before. How'd you know me?'

'I met your daughter and Buster Fenton in town. They're on their way back here now and I wanta surprise them. Something bad is going on between your daughter and Fenton and I need to know what it is.'

'You're mistaken, Deputy.' Ensor grinned. 'Jenny and Buster are fixing to marry soon, and there's always something going on between them. They ain't well matched, so they got problems.' He glanced over his shoulder at the sound of approaching hoofs, and Kendrick looked in the same direction to see the girl and Fenton coming in at a fast clip.

'Lift your gun with finger and thumb and drop it on the ground,' Kendrick said swiftly. 'Make it fast.' He waited until Ensor had complied. 'Now kick it over here.'

Ensor obeyed but there was protest in his expression. 'What in hell is going on?' he demanded. 'You ain't got no right to come in here bracing a man for no reason at all. I got a good name in these parts. I been selling merchandise around Texas for a lot of years. I ain't never been on the wrong side of the law, and that counts for a lot, I guess. I know Abe Lorimer, and he knows me well. He'll tell you I am an honest man.'

'We'll find out in a minute what is going on,' Kendrick replied. 'Your daughter near cracked my skull in town, and if you don't figure that is an offence then you got a poor idea of the law.'

Ensor's face showed a blend of amazement and disbelief, and he shook his head as he watched the approach of the riders. Kendrick stepped to the right to put Ensor between himself and the pair, and crouched a little to conceal his bulk. The pair came into the camp without spotting him, although Fenton stiffened and dropped a hand to his gun butt when he saw Kendrick's black.

'You can lift your gun and throw it into the creek,' Kendrick rasped, stepping out from behind Ensor, his gun muzzle gaping at Fenton's chest. 'And you better sit still and keep your hands on display, sister,' he snapped at the girl.

Fenton stiffened, then lifted his hand slowly from his gun. Jenny Ensor sat motionless, face blank of expression, her blue eyes narrowed and filled with sudden wariness.

'I said to get rid of the gun,' Kendrick rapped, and Fenton, scowling, lifted the weapon gingerly out of leather and flung it into the creek. 'Now get down and put your hands up. Don't even think of giving me trouble. Not you,' he added as the girl prepared to dismount. 'Stay on your horse where I can see you plain, and shuck that rifle before you get any more ideas like the one you had back in the barn.'

The girl discarded the rifle, her taut features showing reluctance. She sat stiffly, her hands on the saddlehorn, her weight resting on them. Defiance gazed at Kendrick from her narrowed eyes.

'That's better.' Kendrick stuck his left leg out to the side to keep undue pressure off it, and the girl spoke as he bent to pick up the rifle.

'What's the matter with your leg?' she demanded.

'I busted it last year,' he responded. 'What's it to you?'

'It should have been your neck,' she retorted, and Fenton chuckled.

'What's been goin' on?' Ensor demanded, looking from his daughter to Fenton and back again. 'I sent you to bring Jenny back, Buster. What have you been up to in town?'

'Nothing.' Fenton shook his head. 'We was minding our own business in the livery barn when this deputy showed up and stuck his nose in. I happened to have my knife in my hand and he figgered I was gonna stick him, or somethin'. He knocked me down, and Jenny laid into him with her rifle butt, so we got out of there pronto.'

Kendrick looked at the girl. 'Buster was threatening you with a knife? So what was going on?'

'It was personal.' She gazed brazenly at Kendrick as she shrugged her slim shoulders. 'And it's none of your business, Deputy.'

'I ought to take the pair of you back to town and let the sheriff deal with you.' Kendrick glanced at Ensor. 'Are you on your way to Clearwater Creek?'

'I was, but now I've changed my mind. We'll head west and run up to Red Mesa. I don't want no trouble, and if these two are spoiling for a fight then it'd better happen in the wide open spaces.'

31

Kendrick gazed at the girl, undecided, and she regarded him calmly, her
face set in angry lines. With his head
aching, and feeling the need of a drink,
he decided to forget about what had
happened in town. Acting on an
impulse, he tossed the rifle under the
wagon.

'I ain't satisfied, not by a long rope,'
he said. 'But I'll give you the benefit of
the doubt this time. You all haul out of
here pronto and keep going until you
hit Red Mesa, and if you ever come
back this way then you better be on
your best behaviour. You got that?'

'Yes, Mr Deputy.' The girl smiled
over-sweetly.

Kendrick's lips tightened as he
fought to curb his temper. Holstering
his pistol, he moved to his horse,
watching the three of them closely, and
climbed into his saddle, favouring his
leg. He did not relax his alertness, and
rode away at a canter with his head
turned to watch them until he was out
of gun range. He saw Ensor begin to

32

remonstrate with the pair, and rode out of sight beyond a ridge.

Once out of their sight, Kendrick dismounted and trailed his reins, then bellied down on the hot ground and crawled back to where he could observe the camp. He saw rapid preparations being made to break camp, and then Ensor got up on the driving-seat of the wagon and cracked his whip, raising dust as he headed out. Fenton grabbed at the girl as soon as the wagon was out of sight but she eluded his clutching hands with practised ease and lunged sideways to snatch up her rifle. Jacking a shell into the breech, she pointed the weapon at Fenton, menacing him with it, and he backed off with waving arms when she jabbed him in the stomach with the muzzle.

Fenton protested and turned away to mount his horse and ride out after the wagon. The girl remained motionless for a couple of moments, then gazed in the direction Kendrick had taken before going to her horse. As she rode away, Kendrick got the feeling that the two of them had performed the same ritual many times. Shaking his head, he dismissed them from his thoughts and went back to his horse.

He mounted and turned back to town, his thoughts turning continually on the situation existing in the county; there were so many imponderables in his mind that he fought shy of facing them. He was fed up to his back teeth with what was happening in the county and having his hands tied by Abe Lorimer. It made him wonder if the sheriff was in league with the badmen. But he knew Lorimer was above that sort of thing. The sheriff was still greatly admired for what he had achieved in the past, fighting against great odds to enforce the law and maintain the peace. He figured that the only problem with Lorimer was that he did not know when it was time to quit. The sheriff was hamstringing the county by hanging on to the reins of office instead of making way for a younger man.

Kendrick rode on at a canter, favouring his left leg by leaning slightly to the right. There were times when he could not even sit a horse because of the pain in his thigh, but today it was almost tolerable, and he was thankful for the job Lorimer had given him because of who his father had been. He pushed through a small herd of long-horns grazing around sparse clumps of buffalo-berry along the banks of the stream, which was fed by the creek he had just left. He glanced around with encompassing gaze. Nothing was moving in the vast extent of cattle range that stretched, seemingly illimitable, towards the imperceptible rise of the northern hills in the far distance.

He sighed irritably when he reached town limits and saw Lorimer still seated on his chair outside the law office. An able sheriff would be in the saddle all hours God made, moving around to check on trouble and ready to deal with it before it could take hold. That was how Lorimer had been in his prime, and it galled Kendrick that the old sheriff's loss of activity contributed greatly to the rise in crime. He dismounted in front of the law office and faced Lorimer, who was regarding him with surprise etched on his craggy face.

'What in hell are you doing back here, Chuck?' he demanded. 'Lord Almighty! When you rode out I thought you was gone for at least a week. What are you doing back here?'

Kendrick dismounted and stood with his weight on his right leg, bending slightly to massage the place where the break had occurred in his left leg. He explained what had happened at the livery barn.

Lorimer shook his head. 'You should have brought them in, considering the trouble we're getting at the moment. I've known Al Ensor a long time, and I ain't happy with what I've heard of his rambling around the state. I reckon he does more than sell pots and pans. I've suspected for a long time that he's been acting as the eyes and ears of the Darra gang.'

'Blink Darra!' Kendrick's eyes glittered. He dropped his hand to the butt of his gun. 'What I wouldn't give to meet up with him! He shot down my dad in cold blood.' He gazed broodingly around the deserted street as if hoping to see Darra riding by. 'If you suspect Ensor then why hasn't he been pulled in?'

'No proof against him.' Lorimer regarded Kendrick's flushed face. 'Are you goin' to visit the Ives place for a spell?'

'I reckon not.' Kendrick shook his head. 'I heard that Sammy Jo is keeping company with Tom Bircham. That's OK by me. I ain't no dog in a manger. If Sammy Jo likes Bircham then I'm happy for her.'

Lorimer sighed and shook his head. He removed his hat and cuffed sweat from his forehead. 'Chuck, go see Clancey and get a sack of supplies for mebbe a week, then take out after Ensor and watch him. It's about time I knew one way or the other what his motives are. If he is working in with the outlaws then he's got to be in close touch with them, and you just might find the link. But no trouble, huh? If you do get the deadwood on Ensor then come back here and tell me about it. You got that? If you go for that crooked bunch bald-headed you'll wind up in a grave next to your pa.'

Kendrick's eyes glinted as he smiled. 'Don't worry about me, Abe. I'll tail Ensor good. I'll be riding out quick, but first I'll take a look at the dodgers you've got on the Darra gang. I've looked at them often enough, but I need to refresh my memory.'

'I'm warning you not to tangle with the gang,' Lorimer insisted.

'Heck, I wouldn't do a fool thing like that!' Kendrick grinned. 'But I want to know what that bunch looks like. If one of them rides in to talk to Ensor while I'm watching then I need to know that he is an outlaw.'

Lorimer agreed grudgingly. Kendrick went into the law office, which was a large room with white-washed adobe walls and had the luxury of pine floorboards. There was a roll-top desk situated under the front window. A gunrack containing several rifles and shotguns was near the door in the back wall that gave access to the cell block, and all the weapons were oiled and cleaned so that the metal parts glinted with a dull bluish sheen. There was a bookshelf near a pot-bellied stove, and a neat row of wanted posters adorned a side wall.

Kendrick crossed to the dodgers and looked at the hard-bitten faces staring out at him. The Darra gang consisted of three permanent members; Blink Darra himself, Trig Weevil and Ike Frayle. Darra was big and arrogant, his character showing in his narrowed eyes. A thin-lipped, cruel mouth did nothing to enhance his appearance, and his reputation went along with his looks.

He was a psychopathic killer who was known to have gunned down a lesser member of his gang for some trivial offence against the code of the bunch, and it was well publicized that he was careless in a shootout; prone to spraying lead into onlookers just for the hell of it. Weevil and Frayle were likewise known for evil deeds, obviously taking their cue from the evil gang boss.

Kendrick studied the three faces although they were already imprinted on the screen of his mind. He had hunted the gang in vain in the days after his father had been killed, but gave up in the face of the blank wall that confronted him whatever way he turned. But he had never lost the desire to see Blink Darra through gunsmoke, aware that his father could not rest easy in his grave until the gang boss had got his just deserts.

He dragged himself from his thoughts, took a last look at the hard faces of the three outlaws, then went back to the street. Lorimer got to his feet, staggering slightly as he did so.

'I'll take a walk along to the store with you,' the sheriff said. 'And we'll keep quiet about what you're going to do. There are too many tongues around town that like to gossip about law business, and if word gets to the wrong ears about your chore you could find yourself in a lot of trouble out there on the range.'

'I'd like the chance to meet Darra,' Kendrick said carelessly. 'So anyone will be doing me a favour by pointing him out to me.'

They walked to the general store and Kendrick procured a sack of provisions. He was eager now to be on his way, and tied the sack behind his cantle. Looking around the street as he swung into his saddle, he was struck by the thought that no one would miss him when he rode out. His was a lonely trail. He touched spurs to the black and cantered away, heading south towards the creek where he had seen the Ensor wagon.

When he reached the creek he paused to look around, thinking of the girl. Jenny Ensor sure had a mean streak. He lifted his hand and explored the painful bump on his skull. That girl didn't seem to have an ounce of appreciation. He had stepped in because he thought Fenton was bothering her and she had rewarded him by near busting his head.

Following the wheel-tracks of the wagon, he rode steadily, watching his surroundings carefully. He could catch up quickly with the wagon, but did not want to advertise the fact that he was trailing the Ensors. An hour later he breasted a rise and saw the wagon rumbling steadily across the range. He turned aside, keeping under cover, and followed from a distance and to the left. If Fenton dropped back at any time to check for tracks he would find a clear trail.

But the chore proved to be boring, and Kendrick's restless nature was such that he soon began to chafe at the slow pace. If Al Ensor made twelve miles a day in that wagon then he would be pushing it. Kendrick sighed for the hundredth time and, acting upon an impulse, swung away to the left, intending to visit Heck Ives at the Triangle I ranch some five miles distant. He had always been friendly with Ives, for the man had been a deputy with his father in the old days, before taking up cattle ranching, and Kendrick was always ready to listen to tales of what law-dealing had been like in the so-called bad old days.

He rode at a fast clip, heading west, and was ascending a long incline barely a mile from Triangle I when his keen eyes picked up the glint of sunlight on metal on the ridge above him. Acting instinctively, he dived out of the saddle and hit the ground hard, the impact sending a shaft of agony through his left leg. But the bullet intended for him missed by a hair's-breadth, and he lay in cover listening to the echoes of the rifle-shot fading away into the illimitable distance.

3

Kendrick lay massaging his leg, teeth clenched against the pain, while his gaze raked the slope above him. He saw a wisp of blue gunsmoke drifting up away from the spot where he had glimpsed the reflection of sunlight on metal, and spotted a faint movement as the ambusher pushed back from his position to depart. Gritting his teeth as yet another twinge of pain surged through his leg, he forced himself upright, muscles tensed for the impact of a bullet, but nothing happened and he lunged for his horse, now grazing quietly.

He dragged his Winchester from its scabbard, jacked a shell into the breech and pushed the weapon across his saddle, drawing a bead on the ambush spot. Moments passed without incident. He finally decided that nothing further was going to happen and climbed back into his saddle to continue up the slope, his rifle covering the ridge. Reining in on the crest, he looked across the undulating range and saw a rider disappearing into cover a hundred yards away. He was too slow for a shot at the man, and saw nothing by which to identify him, except that the horse was dark-coloured, with a circular patch of lighter hair on its left rump.

Cursing his handicap, Kendrick dismounted and cast around for clues, finding an empty cartridge case in the area where the ambusher had fired at him. The cartridge was from a Winchester 44.40, the most popular choice of weapon these days, and he tucked it into a breast pocket. Moving around, he located the spot where the ambusher's horse had stood, and found several clear prints of shod hoofs that had nothing memorable about them.

He considered chasing after the ambusher but the man had a head start, and Kendrick turned again in the direction of Triangle I. His dive from the black had triggered off a niggling pain in his thigh that continued persistently as he rode, and he found partial easement by dismounting and walking for a spell. He was so preoccupied with his condition that he failed to maintain his usual high standard of alertness, and turned swiftly when the sudden rapid beat of several horses approaching sounded from behind, setting alarm flaring in his mind.

Three riders were galloping towards him, bent low in their saddles and urging on their mounts. Kendrick drew his pistol as gunsmoke erupted around the newcomers, and dived for cover as a fusillade of crackling lead raged about him. He rolled into a depression in the grass, his deadly gun lifting readily, but the fire coming at him was too heavy to risk exposure and he crouched low until the shooting eased.

When he finally managed to observe, the trio was almost upon him, and he started shooting. Gunsmoke blew back into his narrowed eyes as he triggered the .45, and he caught the pungent taste of it, like grit between his clenched teeth. His shooting was instinctive but deadly accurate, and his first shot took the rider on the left in the upper chest. The man was swept from his saddle as if a giant hand had struck him. Slugs came back at him from the other two but he continued shooting despite a bullet burn across the top of his left shoulder.

He hit the centre rider and the man slumped over the neck of his horse before pitching sideways out of leather to thump heavily on the grass only feet from where Kendrick was lying. The third man was almost upon him, and Kendrick rolled over on to his back as the horse jumped his position. He had a glimpse of a bearded face peering down at him. The gaping muzzle of a pistol swung to cover him. He fired swiftly. The man uttered a hoarse cry as Kendrick's bullet took him in the left armpit, and went over sideways out of leather, his right foot catching in the stirrup. He was dragged many yards before he became disentangled and lay in an inert heap.

Kendrick had a vague impression that the horse of the third rider resembled the animal of the man who had first ambushed him. He lay motionless on his back, reloading his gun and breathing harshly until the gunsmoke around him dissipated on the stiff breeze. He rubbed his pain-stricken leg to gain relief, then got laboriously to his feet, looking around at the three men lying motionless on the ground. His black had run on several yards and was now grazing quietly.

Kendrick's ears were protesting at the shock of the shooting, and he had to swallow several times before they were cleared of clogging gun thunder. He surveyed his surroundings, looking for more trouble, but the range was now seemingly deserted. He went

48

around the trio, checking them and removing weapons. Two were dead and the third died even as Kendrick bent over him. With his ears still ringing from the shock of gunfire, he sighed heavily and stood back to review the situation.

One of the men had ambushed him at the outset. Kendrick looked at the horse in question and compared it with the fleeting glimpse he had gained of the ambusher disappearing into the brush. Clearly it was the horse the ambusher had ridden, and the man had returned quickly with the other two to finish the job. Curious about the reason behind the attack, he went to his horse, climbed into the saddle, and started back along the tracks the three men had left.

He traced them over the ridge and reined up on the crest to gaze across the range, seeing immediately a small herd of cattle some three hundred yards ahead, being driven west by two men. He sent the black forward to investigate, and, as he approached the herd, one of the drovers spotted him and hurried towards the second man for a discussion. They immediately swung their horses north and rode away at a gallop.

Kendrick closed in on the herd and saw that they were branded Triangle I. With the departure of the drovers, the cattle fell to grazing, and Kendrick gazed at the departing riders, certain now that they were rustlers. He turned and rode back to the scene of the shooting.

Heaving the dead men face down across their saddles, Kendrick rode on to Triangle I, leading the horses and their grisly burdens. It was noon when he looked down on Heck Ives's Triangle I ranch headquarters. Going on, he entered the yard and went to the house.

A girl was sitting on a rocker on the porch of the house, and she got to her feet as Kendrick reached her. Tall and slender, blue-eyed and golden-haired, she was an attractive sight despite the shock that came to her features as she gazed at the three horses Kendrick was leading. Without turning her head or removing her gaze from the dead men, she called an urgent warning that brought Ives himself hurrying out of the house, rifle in hand.

Heck Ives was a man of some fifty years, short and muscular, dressed in good range clothes. Hatless, his fair hair looked as if it had not been combed inside of a month. He paused beside his daughter and gazed silently as Kendrick reined in and dismounted stiffly.

'Howdy, Heck,' Kendrick greeted. 'I met these three on the trail just short of Four Mile Creek.' He explained tersely what had happened.

'Jeez!' Ives came down the porch steps, his face dark with anger. 'I got men out watching the range for rustlers. We ain't been hit before. But I ain't gonna stand by while those coyotes bleed me dry. I heard this morning that Circle B was raided last night, and Bar S was burned to the ground.'

Kendrick nodded. 'Yeah, I was over to Circle B earlier, and got to Bar S in time to see it burning. Slater has taken out after the gang that fired his place and Belmont's got his whole crew out looking for the rustlers.'

'Perhaps that is what we should do,' Ives said thoughtfully. 'If the ranchers got together and worked with one another hunting the rustlers, the range would soon be clean.' He went around the dead men, looking into their faces, shaking his head. 'I never seen any of these before,' he remarked. 'And the buzzards ambushed you, huh? It's come to a pretty pass when a man ain't safe on the trail, Chuck. You go into the house and get something to eat, huh? Sammy Jo, see to Chuck. I'll get the hands together and we'll take out after those two rustlers who high-tailed it. I'll give you ten minutes to get some grub inside you, and you better pack some supplies that I can take along, Sammy Jo.'

'I can't ride with you,' Kendrick said.

'I got a chore to do, and I can't stop even to eat. I had to come in here and warn you what was goin' on, but now I got to be riding. Perhaps you'll send a man to town with these bodies and report to Lorimer what happened.'

'Sure will,' Ives said, and hurried across to the barn.

'You sure you ain't got time to sit and eat?' Sammy Jo demanded. 'I'm feeling a mite lonely today, Chuck, and if Pa rides out with the whole crew I'll be left on my own.'

Kendrick shook his head. 'Sorry. I got to be riding. I've wasted time as it is. And you shouldn't be lonely. I heard tell you're making a good friend of Tom Bircham.'

The girl frowned. 'A girl needs someone for company,' she complained. 'I only see you in a coon's age, and you sure don't want to get friendly with me beyond talking. I don't plan to waste my life, if you do, Chuck Kendrick.'

'I got too much to do as it is,' he retorted. 'I can't complicate things by

53

getting tangled with a gal. So long.'

He touched the brim of his hat with a forefinger and turned to his black, grunting as he climbed into the saddle. Then he rode out without so much as another look at Sammy Jo, heading back to the spot where he had been ambushed. By evening he was hunkered down behind a ridge, looking at Al Ensor making camp by a water hole. Buster Fenton was sitting his horse watching the surrounding range, and Jenny Ensor was collecting buffalo chips for their camp-fire.

Kendrick left his horse in cover on a long rope to enable it to graze. He took his supplies back to his point of vantage and sat eating cold food while watching his quarry eating a hot meal. The sun disappeared beyond the western horizon and long shadows closed in over the range. When darkness finally settled, Kendrick walked down the slope towards the lonely camp, where a fire glowed dimly, and dropped to the ground and crawled forward until he was close enough to hear voices. But he was out of luck. He had hardly got into position when the girl climbed into the wagon to sleep and the two men rolled into their blankets under the wagon.

Kendrick lay motionless until both men were asleep, then returned to his own camp. He unsaddled the black and turned in himself, dropping off to sleep almost instantly and arising before the sun showed next morning. He was saddled and ready to travel long before the Ensors broke camp, and when he went forward to check their progress he discovered that Buster Fenton was not there, and the man's horse was gone.

Kendrick cursed soundly as he watched the wagon pull out, Ensor driving the team and Jenny walking beside the wagon, her horse tied behind. He waited until they had disappeared before riding down the slope to the campsite. There he saw tracks leading out to the west. The trail was faint, but he could tell by crushed blades of grass and slight indentations that a horse had travelled through. Knowing that he could always catch up with the wagon, he took out after Fenton, riding slowly, his attention centred on the poor trail.

Fenton had headed west, and Kendrick racked his brains trying to work out where the man could be heading. There were ranches ahead, and a trading post at Twin Forks, a village some ten miles ahead. Kendrick nodded. Twin Forks it seemed to be. But he kept a close eye on the faint trail as he rode in case Fenton was headed somewhere else, and he was not suprised when the tracks led straight to the half-dozen habitations huddled together at the meeting of four trails.

Kendrick reined in when he saw Twin Forks. There were five saddle horses standing at the tie rail outside the single-storey trading post, and a Wells Fargo coach, minus its team, was out front. Kendrick wondered what the passengers were doing: five of them standing beside the coach with their hands raised in the air. Three men were standing around the passengers, and then Kendrick saw guns on display and his jawline tightened as realization hit him. The coach was being robbed!

He jerked his Winchester from its scabbard and cocked it, lifting the weapon to his shoulder. There had been a spate of coach robberies in the county in the past six months. He estimated the range at 150 yards, and aimed at a fourth man, who was standing on top of the coach in the act of lifting the strongbox. Squeezing the trigger, he was shifting his aim to the other hold-up men when the man atop the coach jerked and spun, then fell to the roof and bounced off to lie inertly in the dust behind the vehicle.

The three robbers surrounding the passengers froze in shock as the crash of the shot echoed to the horizon. Kendrick fired swiftly, taking the man on the right and shifting his aim before his shot struck home. But as the man crumpled, the remaining two recovered from their shock and went running for their horses. Kendrick downed another before he reached the waiting animals, and the fourth man was swinging into his saddle when a slug from Kendrick's deadly rifle tore through his right shoulder blade.

Kendrick exhaled sharply as gun-smoke clogged his lungs. He went forward at a canter, and none of the passengers moved until he reached the coach. Then his law star was spotted and sight of it broke the shock holding the group. Four men and a woman crowded around Kendrick as he dismounted, and all began talking at once. Kendrick saw two men lying motionless in the dust on the far side of the coach and shrugged off the passengers.

He gazed grim-eyed at the driver and shotgun guard lying in the dust. Both were dead, and he had known them well. They had been on the regular run through the county. He turned away and went around the hold-up men, checking them, removing their guns.

Three were dead, the one by the horses in front of the trading post lying unconscious, badly wounded.

Kendrick turned to the passengers and quickly learned what had happened. The robbers had concealed themselves in the trading post until the team was removed from the coach. Then they struck, shooting down the driver and the guard without warning. Kendrick turned to the trading post to see the proprietor, Huff Stafford, standing in the doorway, and Buster Fenton was beside him.

'These robbers were hiding in your place,' Kendrick observed, his keen gaze on Fenton. 'Tell me about it, Stuff.'

'Sure they were. But they acted like ordinary cowpokes. They had a beer apiece, and some food. I didn't know what they were up to until the coach pulled in, and then there was nothing I could do. They would have killed me in cold blood, like they did the driver and the guard.'

'And where were you when this was happening?' Kendrick asked Fenton.

'I came here to pick up some supplies Ensor was needing, and these guys told me not to butt in or I'd stop lead.' Fenton seemed shocked. 'I never saw anything like your shooting, Deputy. Four shots in four seconds and four men down in the dust. I'm sure glad I didn't tangle with you back in Clearwater Creek. What are you doin' here, turning up just in time to stop a coach hold-up?'

'I tangled with some rustlers near Triangle I — killed three of them. Two got away, and I was following their tracks in this direction. Has there been a couple of long riders through here today, Stuff?'

Stafford shook his head. He was a large, overweight man of untidy appearance, wearing stained clothes, and looking as if his last bath had been at the hands of a midwife. Unshaven, his unkempt beard covered an ugly face. His nose was misshapen, bulbous at the end, and his pale eyes were slitted and mean, which went along with his reputation for being an unscrupulous cheat.

'Fenton is the only one to show up around here today,' he growled. 'Apart from the robbers, that is. I don't know what this place is comin' to. It's getting so an honest man is afraid to close his eyes at night.'

'I better get moving,' Fenton interposed. 'I got to get back to the wagon,'

He stepped out of the doorway and started towards his tethered horse, until Kendrick put a restraining hand on his arm as he passed.

'You came here for supplies, didn't you?' Kendrick asked. 'Where are they?'

Fenton's face hardened and his eyes narrowed. 'Hell,' he rapped. 'The robbery knocked it clean out of my mind.' He laughed inanely. 'Jenny would give me hell if I showed up without the supplies. Sack up some bacon and beans, Stuff, and I'll split the breeze.'

Kendrick remained in the doorway of the trading post while Stafford and Fenton went inside. He was wondering what Fenton's real reason was for riding in. But speculation was useless in this situation, and he turned to the four horses the robbers had ridden. A search of their saddle-bags revealed nothing, and he went around the men again, gazing into their dead faces, hoping to recognize at least one of them, perhaps to tie them into one of the big gangs. He came to the fourth man, who died as he bent over him, and shook his head in frustration as he straightened.

Fenton emerged from the trading post, touched his hat to Kendrick, and grinned insolently as he tied a small gunny sack behind his cantle. He swung into his saddle, and Kendrick watched him ride away before turning to Stafford, who had resumed his position in the doorway.

'Have you got a man who can take the coach on to the the next relay station?' he asked.

'Yeah.' Stafford nodded. 'Don't worry about it. Dan Fowler runs the station here — a Wells Fargo man. He'll take care of the passengers, if the robbers didn't kill him.'

Kendrick nodded and turned away. He climbed into his saddle and rode off, careful to head in the opposite direction to the one Fenton had taken, but when he was out of sight of the trading post he swung east and angled back to pick up Fenton's trail. His thoughts were busy, clouded with suspicion. Had Fenton really ridden miles across the range just to pick up a small sack of supplies? Surely a man of Al Ensor's experience wouldn't run out of essential supplies between towns. So what had been Fenton's real purpose? Was it coincidence that he arrived at the trading post just before the hold-up? Or did his errand have a more sinister explanation? Was he connected in any way with the robbers? Abe Lorimer had voiced suspicions about Ensor, suspecting the man of having dealings with the Darra gang.

Kendrick followed Fenton's trail, staying well back, alert for any sudden move the man might make. But Fenton rode steadily, not once looking over his shoulder, and Kendrick was tired and aching by the time his quarry caught up with the Ensor wagon. He was thankful when Ensor made camp at Fenton's appearance, and dismounted to eat cold food while, over the ridge, Jenny Ensor cooked a hot meal on the little camp-fire.

The day was almost over. The sun was low in the west, the breeze strengthening. Kendrick lay on his belly watching the camp, and just before the sun finally disappeared below the horizon he went back to his horse and unsaddled it for the night. Returning to the crest for a final look at the camp, he was shocked by the sight of three riders dismounting beside the wagon.

Voices came to him faintly through the dusk, and Kendrick cursed himself for not being fully alert. He dropped to the ground and crawled towards the wagon, moving slowly and awkwardly, his left leg stuck out in an attempt to ease his pain, and he tried to control his impatience. He squinted his eyes to get a look at the newcomers, but it was now too dark for vision and the camp-fire was merely a dull red glow in the shadows.

But Kendrick could hear the voices that carried easily through the night. He recognized Ensor's voice, and the raised tone of Jenny Ensor as someone called her out of the wagon to make a fresh pot of coffee. The girl was in an abrasive mood, and her sharp voice raised a laugh among the newcomers.

'What in hell happened at the trading post, Fenton?' one of the men demanded. 'You better have a good reason why the deal was fouled up.'

'Chuck Kendrick is the reason,' Fenton replied hoarsely.

'Who in hell is he?'

'A deputy sheriff from Clearwater Creek,' Ensor cut in. 'I've met him. His pa was Sam Kendrick, the town marshal at Bleak Ridge some years back. You must remember Kendrick! He stopped Blink and the boys taking the bank there about twelve years ago.'

'Yeah. I remember him. Trig gunned him down. The derned coot didn't know when to quit. He sure was hell on wheels.'

Kendrick clenched his teeth as he listened. Trig gunned down his father! Trig would be Trig Weevil, one of the foremost of the Darra bunch. And these men had to be a part of that gang. He reached for his sixgun, and had to struggle with his conscience before he could resist the temptation to throw lead at the hardcases. He consoled himself with the knowledge that his time would come. All he had to do right now was follow the sheriff's instructions, and, despite his apparent idleness, Abe Lorimer seemed to be hitting the nail on the head yet again. He had a finger on the pulse of the county, and Kendrick knew he could not afford to miss this opportunity to get the dead-wood on the outlaws. Lorimer's hunch had put him right in for the gang.

'By the sound of it, we're gonna have to put a kink in the tail of this Kendrick,' one of the outlaws said. 'You got any idea where he headed after the trading post?'

'I didn't wait around to learn his plans,' Fenton retorted. 'I moved out of there fast, and didn't stop until I got back here. But you're sure gonna have to do something about him before he runs you all ragged.'

'We're heading back to the hideout after we've dropped in at the trading post. It'll be up to Blink what happens to the deputy. Mebbe he'll send Trig out to nail him, huh?'

The others laughed, and Kendrick clenched his hands as he fought against the impulse to launch himself into action. For several tense moments he was on the brink of losing his control and cutting loose with his deadly gun, but common sense prevailed and he sneaked away to prepare his horse for travelling. If those three outlaws were going back to Darra's hideout then he wanted to be on their tail when they reached it.

By the time he returned to his vantage point the three long riders were swinging into their saddles.

'Don't forget, Buster, Blink wants the dope on that bank in South Creek, and he wants it quick. I reckon it's next on the list. We'll meet up with you in five days at the old McKinley ranch over in Benson County. Will you be there?'

'Sure will,' Fenton replied, 'and I'll have the details on the bank.' He laughed. 'You boys better keep your eyes skinned after this. There ain't no telling when Chuck Kendrick might cross your trail.'

The three men swung into their saddles and rode off into the night. Kendrick went back to his horse and climbed wearily into the saddle, aware that he would get no rest before dawn. He made no attempt to follow the trio for he knew their destination, and took a slightly longer route in order to avoid running into them. But he wanted to be on their trail when they rode into Blink Darra's hideout.

Dawn found him hunkered down on a ridge overlooking the trading post. He was tired and hungry, but there was a leaping eagerness inside him as he considered his chances of locating Darra's lair, and facing Trig Weevil, who had shot down his father in cold blood.

The three outlaws were inside the post, probably regaling themselves with food and coffee, and Kendrick ate cold food and waited for them to reappear. He did not care how long he had to wait or what discomforts lay ahead if he could eventually get to the Darra gang.

The sound of a group of riders approaching aroused him and he turned quickly to see half a dozen tough cowpunchers with Frank Belmont at their head cantering towards the trading post. The Circle B rancher had been out looking for rustlers, and

Kendrick uttered a groan as he imagined what would happen if the cowhands came face to face with the outlaws. But there was nothing he could do without revealing his presence, and he kept low and watched through narrowed eyes.

The Circle B crew dismounted in front of the trading post and tethered their mounts. And then it happened. As they trooped towards the door a sixgun inside the post smashed the glass in a front window and began shooting indiscriminately into them.

4

Kendrick watched in disbelief as Frank Belmont and the Circle B outfit rushed the trading post. Gunshots blasted and echoes fled across the range. One puncher took a slug in the chest and fell to the ground. The others entered, and shooting increased for interminable seconds, then shut off. A heavy silence settled after the echoes had faded. Kendrick sighed as he fetched his horse. He mounted and rode down to the squat adobe building.

Kendrick dismounted at the door, trailed his reins and went into the trading post. The interior was filled with drifting gunsmoke, and four figures were sprawled on the floor, Stuff Stafford, the trader, among them. Frank Belmont was standing by the bar, a whiskey bottle in his hand. He was in the act of wiping his mouth with the back of a hand. He caught Kendrick's movement and whirled around, gun muzzle swinging.

'Hold it,' Kendrick said quickly. 'You've just ruined my play, Frank. I was watching those three, hoping they'd lead me to Blink Darra's hideout.'

'Darra? How'd he get into this?' The Circle B rancher holstered his gun and looked around. He was tall and thin, middle-aged, with a lean, weather-beaten face and piercing blue eyes. 'Are these men outlaws? I figgered them for rustlers. They started shooting at us the minute we dismounted. We've been chasing a bunch of cattle-thieves all day, and they was headed in this direction.'

'You must have crossed trails some-where and came on here.' Kendrick could see at a glance that the trio he had been following were dead. 'I trailed these three from the east, and they must have figured you for a posse. What about Stafford? Did he side against you?'

'He pulled a gun so I let him have it. I've thought for some time that he's been giving information to the long riders passing through. Mebbe he was working with the rustlers.'

'That's the way I got it figured.' Kendrick nodded. He explained the incidents that had befallen him, and Belmont grimaced as he took another swig from the whiskey bottle.

'You have been busy! And you pulled off more than we have. So rustlers are hitting everyone in the county! We ranchers are gonna have to get together to stop the rot that's set in on this range. I reckon we're just wasting our time, following trails that lead nowhere.'

Kendrick checked the men lying on the floor, finding, as he suspected, that they were dead. Reaching Stafford, who was dead also, he stood looking down at the big figure, trying to get a picture of what had been happening around here. The coach hold-up earlier made sense now, with Stafford being implicated, and that led Kendrick's thoughts to

Buster Fenton. His eyes narrowed as he considered. Fenton would have a lot of explaining to do the next time their trails crossed.

'Frank, take these bodies into town and report the shooting to the sheriff,' he said briskly, filled with a growing desire to get to grips with his problems. 'Tell him I'm on the job. I have to be riding now.'

Kendrick crossed the big room to where Stafford kept his guns and cartridges and helped himself to two boxes of ammunition: one for his Colt pistol and the other for the Winchester. He departed, riding back the way he had come. It was time he had a showdown with Al Ensor and Buster Fenton. They had to be working in with the outlaws, and he would get at the truth if he had to knock it out of them.

It was almost nightfall when he caught up with the Ensor wagon, which was now close to the little town nestling in the shadow of Red Mesa, from which it took its name. It wasn't much of a town, just a short straggle of adobe buildings along the trail which housed the community living out here in the back of the beyond. There was a bank, a livery barn, a blacksmith's shop, two saloons, and a small general store catering for the frugal needs of the one hundred or so townsfolk.

Kendrick watched from cover as Ensor took the wagon to the back of the livery barn. He watched Fenton hurry off to the nearest saloon while Ensor took care of the team. Jenny Ensor got into the wagon in her trail clothes, and emerged after having changed into a red dress. Kendrick gazed at her with some interest, wondering why she was bothering with her appearance in such a remote spot.

The girl departed without a word to her father, and Kendrick curbed his impatience as he waited for nightfall. The sky was already darkening to the east. When full dark came, he rode on into Red Mesa and put the black in the livery barn, taking care of the animal's needs before turning his thoughts to himself.

He found an eating-house and ate a big meal, trying to relax and unwind from the rigours of the day. Afterwards he went into one of the saloons and bought a beer, drinking it with relish, his eyes busy as he stood alone at a corner of the bar. He spotted Buster Fenton at a card-table across the room, engaged in conversation with a shifty-eyed, sharp-faced man who was wearing two guns on crossed cartridge belts. The stranger looked as if he had never done an honest day's work in his life, and interested Kendrick immediately.

Fenton soon spotted Kendrick, and leaned across the table to say something in the other man's ear. Kendrick saw the man turn his head sharply in his direction and subject him to a pro-longed stare. He let his gaze slide away from the pair, but did not lose sight of them. A few minutes later, Fenton arose and departed, pausing at the batwings to glance in Kendrick's direction. He grinned and departed, and Kendrick called for another beer, feeling the need to cut the trail dust lining his throat.

Later, Kendrick left the saloon and walked to the hotel to get a room, followed by the man Fenton had been talking to. The man stood in the lobby of the hotel until Kendrick went to his room. As soon as he was in the room, Kendrick locked the door. He went to the window, opened it, climbed out and moved through the shadows towards the front door of the building. He saw Fenton's acquaintance questioning the hotel clerk, and when the man emerged, Kendrick followed him along the street.

The man went to the livery barn and fetched out a horse. As he swung into his saddle, Kendrick stepped forward out of the shadows and grasped the bridle.

'What the hell?' the man demanded, reaching for his right-hand gun.

Kendrick blocked the move and dragged the man out of leather, sledging his right fist against his jaw.

The horse cavorted, moving away, and Kendrick supported the unconscious figure while he removed the guns from the man's holsters and tossed them away into the darkness. He lifted the man bodily, carried him to the nearby water trough, and pushed his head into the stagnant water, holding it there until he struggled for air.

'You've been following me,' Kendrick said. 'What's your name, mister? Then tell me about your connection with Buster Fenton, and why I interest you.'

'I'm Jake Wiley. I don't know anyone called Buster Fenton, and I never saw you before in my life. I sure as hell ain't got no interest in you. What's the idea, dousing me in that trough?'

'So you wanta play it tough, huh?' Kendrick nodded. 'That's fine by me. But I ain't got time for games right now. I'll jail you until I got more time. Come on. I expect you know where the law office is. Head for it, and don't make the mistake of trying to jump me or you'll wind up dead. Now get moving.'

He thrust Wiley towards the street. The man seemed unwilling to obey, but he was like a child beside Kendrick and walked hesitantly along the street. Kendrick remained a couple of paces behind, pistol in his hand, and did not relax his attention. They came to the law office, a small building next to the bank, and Wiley thrust open the door and entered. He stopped before a desk, behind which sat Deke Hamley, the deputy sheriff of Red Mesa, who looked up quickly from the mail-order catalogue he was scanning.

'What in hell do you want, Wiley?' Hamley growled. He was a big man, tall and powerfully built, but looked undersized compared to Kendrick. His blue eyes held a bullying glitter in their depths and his fleshy face wore a habitual expression which compressed his lips. He reminded Kendrick of a weasel. His lips curved in a grin of anticipation as he regarded Wiley, and then his gaze shifted to Kendrick's big figure and his manner changed abruptly.

'Chuck,' he said. 'What are you doin' here? Have you come to relieve me? I'm sick of being tucked away in this one-horse burg. When I saw Lorimer last week, he promised me a change.'

'I'm just passing through,' Kendrick replied coolly. He had never liked Hamley, who was noted for question-able tactics in dispensing the law. 'Toss this guy behind bars until I can get back to him.'

'What have you been up to, Wiley?' Hamley grinned and flexed his thick fingers. 'You haven't been stupid, have you? Step on Kendrick's toes and he'll stomp you, but good. All right. You know where the cells are. Turn your pockets out on the desk, then go through to the back.'

Wiley obeyed. Hamley picked up a bunch of keys and followed the man to the back of the office, where a heavy door gave access to the cells. Kendrick followed, and stepped close to the cell when Hamley had locked Wiley in.

'What did Fenton tell you about me?' he demanded. 'You followed me afterwards.'

'I don't know what you're talking about.' Wiley shook his head. 'Like I said, I never saw you before in my life.'

'Is Fenton in town?' Hamley demanded. 'I thought I'd scared him off the last time he came through here. What's he doing back?'

'That's what I intend to find out.' Kendrick reached through the bars and grasped Wiley's shirt, dragging the man so close to the bars that his face was pressed painfully against them. 'I ain't in the mood for games,' he rapped. 'You'll loosen up if you know what's good for you.'

'I'll have a talk with him when you leave,' Hamley said with a grin. 'I got nuthin' to keep me amused. Drop by later, Chuck. Wiley will be eager to talk when I get through with him.'

'Leave him be until I get back,'

Kendrick warned. He departed, and paused on the street to look around the little town. He knew most of the folks who lived here, but none was a close friend. He walked back to the saloon and peered in over the batwings, looking for Fenton, but the man was not around. Then he saw Al Ensor at a corner of the bar, drinking beer, and entered to go to the pedlar's side.

Ensor seemed to be thoughtful, and started nervously when he glanced sideways and saw Kendrick at his elbow.

'Hi, Deputy,' he greeted. 'Buy you a drink?'

'No thanks.' Kendrick shook his head. 'Where's Fenton? He was in here earlier.'

'I ain't set eyes on him since he left me at the wagon.' Ensor shrugged. 'What do you want him for?'

'Some unfinished business.' Kendrick spoke casually. 'I'll catch up with him later. Where's your daughter?'

'How in hell would I know? She's old

enough to mind her own business, and that's what she's always done. Never talks to me about anything. Is she in some kind of trouble?'

'Probably, if she's hanging around with Fenton. Do you have much business in town?'

'A fair bit. I usually sell some pots and pans around here.'

'Where do you go when you leave here?'

'Probably head north. Ain't covered that area in a couple of years. But I'm getting a mite too old for travellin'. I'm thinking of quitting and settling down someplace.'

'I can't believe that.' Kendrick shook his head. 'You've been on the trail all your life. You couldn't leave it now.'

'Mebbe you're right at that. But it ain't the same any more. Times are changing, and I reckon a wise man would get out of the business.'

Kendrick moved away. Not needing a drink, he shook his head when the bartender caught his eye. He left the saloon and walked through the rutted dust of the wide street. The sound of hoofs hammered somewhere behind him and he moved instinctively towards the nearest wall for cover. A rider went by like a bat out of hell and pulled his horse to a slithering halt in front of the law office, then sprang from the saddle and ran into the office without pausing to hitch his mount. Kendrick gazed at the lighted window of the jail and wondered what Hamley was learning that was so urgent.

He was still motionless in the shadows when a man and a woman emerged from the building where he was standing and passed within feet of him. Lamplight from a nearby window fell upon the woman's features, and Kendrick frowned as he recognized Jenny Ensor, for she was holding the arm of her male companion, who was a stranger to Kendrick.

The pair went to the restaurant, and Kendrick followed, watching from the shadows until they had entered the building, then peering through a window to observe them. They sat down at a corner table, the girl with her left profile to the window, the man sitting opposite. Kendrick studied the man's face. He was at least forty-five, dressed in a dark-blue store suit, his appearance neat and professional. Kendrick had never seen him before, and thought he looked like a cattle-buyer. The two ordered supper. Jenny Ensor was in a good mood, nodding and laughing at her companion's conversation, and talking animatedly in her turn.

Kendrick wondered where Fenton was, for Jenny seemed like a woman who was in the company of the man she loved, and yet she was supposed to be on the point of marrying Fenton. He let his keen gaze drift over the other diners in the big room, and stiffened when he spotted Fenton seated at another table with a man who had about him all the earmarks of a long rider.

What was going on? The question

loomed in Kendrick's mind. He noted that Fenton was glancing in Jenny's direction every other moment, but didn't look like a man whose intended was acting like a young lover besotted with her beau. At that moment, Fenton got to his feet and came towards the door, followed by his hard-bitten companion. He smiled at the girl and her companion and departed. Kendrick faded back into the shadows and, when Fenton and his companion went along the street, he followed them at a distance, his thoughts buzzing with contemplation. He was struck by the thought that there was something familiar about the face of the man accompanying Fenton, and it niggled at him.

Fenton and his companion went straight to the law office and entered. Kendrick stood in the shadows beside the big front window of the office and peered inside. Hamley was seated at his desk, alone now, and Kendrick wondered where the rider who had arrived so hurriedly a short time before had gone. He saw Fenton and the other man approach the desk, and was surprised when Fenton sat down nonchalantly on a corner of it, swinging a leg and grinning at the big deputy. They seemed so friendly, but Kendrick knew Hamley as a man who did not encourage friendship under any guise.

He wished he could hear what was being said, but had to be content with studying expressions and demeanour. Hamley was grinning forcedly, nodding while Fenton talked at some length. But then the mood of the meeting changed abruptly. Hamley's smile faded. Fenton suddenly drew his gun and pushed the muzzle to within an inch of the deputy's nose, waggling it slightly. Hamley froze, shaking his head emphatically, his expression tense. Fenton eased his gun forward until the muzzle enclosed the tip of Hamley's nose. He said something sharply, then holstered his gun abruptly and stood up, wagging a finger in Hamley's face. He grinned at his silent companion and they departed.

Kendrick faded back into the shadows and stood with his right hand resting on the butt of his holstered gun while the two men passed him and went along the street. When they entered the saloon he stood undecided for a moment, wondering whether he should maintain a watch on them, confront Hamley, or go back to the restaurant and observe Jenny Ensor and her companion.

His mind was diverted by the sound of a shot erupting in the saloon, and he ran along the street as the echoes faded sullenly through the shadows. Reaching the batwings, he peered over them, and saw Fenton and his companion standing against the bar, their hands raised. A tall man dressed in range clothes was holding a gun in his hand, a faint wisp of gunsmoke curling from the muzzle. Kendrick heard running footsteps coming fast towards the saloon and, acting on an impulse, stepped back into the shadows. Deke Hamley arrived like a runaway horse and barged through the batwings without even pausing to peer into the big room.

Kendrick looked through a window and saw the man with the gun swinging around to face Hamley. The big deputy did not pause in his stride, and when he reached the man's side he made a grab for the levelled gun and snatched it out of the man's hand. Without pausing, he slammed the barrel against the man's head, felling him instantly. Then he turned on Fenton and began to tongue-lash him, his manner now entirely different from the way he had acted in his office.

When Hamley paused for breath he motioned to the man on the floor, and Fenton and his companion picked up the hardcase and emerged from the saloon with him. They headed back to the jail, carrying the man, with Hamley following closely behind.

Kendrick shook his head, perplexed by the behaviour of all concerned. But it was not his business how Hamley handled the law in Red Mesa. He went back to the restaurant to check on Jenny Ensor, and was surprised to see that she and her companion had been joined by two range-clad men who looked as if they had just finished trying to drink one of the saloons dry. The man nearest the girl was holding her by one shoulder, and she was struggling to break the grip while her cattle-buyer acquaintance sat motionless and taut-faced.

Kendrick entered the restaurant and paused beside the girl's table. He looked around, studying the scene.

'Miss Ensor,' he said quietly, 'is this man bothering you?'

The man's head slewed round and he looked up at Kendrick, his hard features showing a scowl.

'Beat it, mister,' he rasped, and glanced at his companion. 'See him off, Zeke.'

The second man pushed back his chair and started to his feet. Kendrick palmed his gun and slammed it against the man's skull. There was a choked-off groan and the man subsided to the floor. Kendrick aimed a blow with his gun barrel at the wrist of the hardcase holding the girl, breaking his hold. The man surged up from the table, uttering a string of curses, and Kendrick stuck the muzzle of his gun into a hard, lean stomach. The man froze and looked into Kendrick's eyes.

'So what's going on here?' Kendrick demanded. 'I asked if this man was bothering you, Miss Ensor.'

'He's not bothering me,' she replied stiffly. 'He's my father's friend, and just a bit high-spirited. This is his idea of having fun. He wasn't harming me.'

Kendrick frowned, preferring to believe his eyes rather than Jenny's words, but if she was not making a complaint there was nothing he could do about it.

'Who are you, mister?' he demanded.

'None of your business,' came the reply. 'Wearing that star don't give you the right to stick your nose into my business.'

Kendrick smiled. 'Conduct that's likely to lead to a breach of the peace is my business,' he retorted. 'You were handling the lady, and I don't stand for that sort of thing whether she minds or not. And you ordered your sidekick to see me off, which he seemed keen to do. I reckon the both of you should see the inside of the jail, so get rid of your gun and let's get moving.'

'You shouldn't do that,' Jenny said heavily. 'It'll just make trouble for you.' She glanced at her silent companion, hesitated, then added, 'This is Arch Kington, a big cattle-buyer from Abilene. These two men are part of the crew hired to drive to Kansas any cattle that Arch buys down here. They won't be around long. Give yourself a break and forget about this. I'm not making a complaint, so forget about it. There was no harm done, so don't pile up trouble for yourself.'

Kendrick regarded Jenny's face. She

was almost pleading with him, and it was the first time he had seen her without a chip on her shoulder. He wondered what she had against lawmen in general and him in particular. He nodded.

'OK,' he said. 'It's against my better judgement, but I'll overlook it this time.' He glared at the man he was covering with his gun. 'You better pull in your horns, mister, or you'll find yourself in big trouble, and that goes for your sidekick too. I'll be watching you while I'm in town, so don't even look like stepping out of line.'

He holstered his gun and departed, stalking out of the restaurant, and slammed the door at his back. Pausing in the shadows, he looked around, wondering why he was letting Jenny get her way. But he intended being around to watch developments, and set off for the law office, wanting to get a line on Hamley's behaviour.

When he entered the office he was surprised to see the deputy sitting quietly at his desk with no sign of Fenton and the other men. Hamley looked up at him, his face showing displeasure at Kendrick's presence.

'You still nosing around?' Hamley demanded. 'What are you doing around here, anyway? Did Lorimer send you to check up on me?'

'Why should he want to do that?' Kendrick was reminding himself that he did not like Hamley. The man was a bully — little better than any of the men he arrested for being drunk and disorderly. There had been complaints about the way he was handling the law in Red Mesa, and Kendrick remembered being surprised when Lorimer had not taken this man to task over his behaviour.

'I ain't happy with the way Lorimer ties down us deputies,' Hamley complained. 'We're like dogs on a leash. We ain't permitted to investigate crimes like deputies in other places do. I'm getting tired of it, and I'm thinking of getting out. It seems to me that

Lorimer doesn't want to catch the criminals we know are around. What do you think about that?'

Kendrick thought of his own attempts to get out from under Lorimer's wing. He shook his head. There was a lot wrong with the law-dealing in this county and he knew that a big shake-up was needed to straighten it out. But he had no idea who was causing the foul-up or what had to be done to put matters right. He shook his head.

'It's no use asking me about it,' he said tersely. 'Take it up with Lorimer.'

'I'd have to go to Clearwater Creek to do that and I can't get away from here right now. So what are you doing in this neck of the woods?'

'Trailing some suspects.'

'Who are they and what are they suspected of? Are they here in Red Mesa?'

'Lay off. I'll handle my chores in my own way. You look like you've got your hands full on your own account. What kind of a hold has Buster Fenton got on you?'

'Fenton? What the hell are you talking about? I ran Fenton out of town the last time I saw him.'

'He seemed to own the place when he was in here a few minutes ago.' Kendrick held Hamley's gaze, and saw wariness seep into the man's pale eyes. 'What was that business about with his gun? He had you looking down the barrel, and it was plain to see that he was warning you off something.'

'It's his way of joking, and I couldn't do anything about it while Cal Pearson was backing him.' Hamley glared at Kendrick. 'But I'll teach him some manners the next time I see him.'

'Who is Cal Pearson? He looks like a bad 'un to me. Why do you let men like him stay in town?'

'You can't go by looks. He's rough, I know, but there's a big cattle-buyer from Abilene in town and Pearson is ramrodding his outfit. They're all tough men, but they're bringing business to Red Mesa. Now why don't you get out of here and leave me to handle my own chores? I don't need you sticking your nose in.'

'You'll never change, Hamley,' Kendrick said. 'You're a poor excuse for a lawman, and I'm tempted to put you behind bars. I've had a look around town, and the place is crowded with hardcases. There are so many of them they're falling over each other.'

'Tend to your own business,' Hamley snarled. 'I don't need you coming in here treating me like trash. Who in hell do you think you are? I've had just about enough of you, so you better up stakes and get to hell out of here before I forget I'm wearing a star.'

'I'll make a report to Lorimer when I get back to Clearwater Creek,' Kendrick said, 'and if you've got an ounce of sense you'll be long gone from here by the time the sheriff comes to investigate.'

'You damn' interfering buzzard!' Hamley sprang to his feet and clawed out his gun, his eyes blazing with hatred.

Kendrick was taken by surprise but reacted instinctively. He drew his gun fast, and the law office erupted in a raucous blasting of gunsmoke and hot lead.

5

Kendrick was shocked by Hamley's action. Taken by surprise, he started his draw a split second behind the deputy, but his superior speed brought his gun into the aim before Hamley could cock his weapon. Kendrick fired as his muzzle lined up on Hamley's chest. The blasting crash of the shot shook the office. Hamley was levelling his gun when Kendrick's big .45 slug struck him. He jerked under the impact and fell back into his seat, his trigger finger squeezing off a shot that bored harmlessly into the top of the desk. Blood spurted as he slid sideways off the chair and crumpled on the floor, his convulsive trigger finger firing a second shot that missed Kendrick's left shoulder by a hair's-breadth and embedded itself in the street door.

Ears ringing, Kendrick gazed down

at the deputy while he fought down his shock. He holstered his gun and dropped to one knee beside Hamley. The deputy was dead, and Kendrick let his thoughts rove over the incidents that had occurred since his arrival in Red Mesa. He now needed to talk to Buster Fenton and get an explanation from him of what had passed during his confrontation with Hamley. Knowing the kind of man Hamley was, Fenton's attitude when he visited the office had been greatly surprising. Hamley had seemed afraid of Fenton, yet he boasted of running Fenton out of town on a previous encounter.

The street door was thrust open and a short, fat man, whose fleshy face was alive with curiosity, came bustling into the office. Doc McKee, in his middle fifties, was dressed in a brown store-suit, and wore a black string tie which caused the flesh of his neck to bulge over his collar. He came to the desk as Kendrick regained his feet.

'Chuck,' McKee observed. 'I didn't

know you were in town. Where's Hamley? I was passing the office when I heard the shot and wondered what the hell he was doing.' He caught sight of Hamley's outflung hand behind the desk and craned forward for a better look. 'Jeez!' he gasped, and pushed past Kendrick to examine the deputy. Then he arose and stood looking into Kendrick's grimly set face. 'He's beyond my help,' he observed. 'What in hell happened?'

'That's what I have to find out,' Kendrick rasped. 'Hamley drew on me without warning, but wasn't quick enough by half.' He fingered the bullet hole in the desk. 'Get Pete Sanchez to take care of the body, Doc. I got things to do.'

'Sure.' McKee's face was a picture of shocked disbelief. 'I always thought Hamley was playing his cards close to his vest, and some of his acquaintances were doubtful, to say the least. I reckoned he was gonna get himself shot one day, but not by one of his colleagues.'

'I'll talk to you later,' Kendrick promised. 'Perhaps you'll be able to shed a little light on Hamley's recent activities. He sure had me guessing tonight, and I know what you mean about the men he mixed with. I need to get hold of a couple of them right now.'

He turned abruptly and left the office, having to push through the gathering townsmen who had been attracted by the shots. Ignoring the questions flung at him, he hurried along the street, looking for Buster Fenton. He checked the saloon. Al Ensor was still at the bar, but there was no sign of Fenton.

Kendrick searched through the town, but Fenton had vanished as if spirited away. But he could be in any of a dozen private residences, and short of making a house to house search, there was no way of unearthing him. Kendrick went to the stable, his hand close to the butt of his gun as he entered the dim interior. Fenton's horse was not there. Kendrick stood in the shadows, blaming himself for being sidetracked by the events of the evening. He should have realized at the outset that Fenton was the crucial figure in the business evolving behind the scenes in the town.

But even Jenny Ensor was implicated in what was going on. She had met Arch Kington in town as if by arrangement, and yet she could have had no idea of his presence when she left the wagon at the back of the stable, having donned a dress apparently in anticipation of entertaining the cattle-buyer.

Kendrick went to the back door of the barn and peered out at the Ensor wagon. He saw the faint red glow of a dying camp-fire, and two knee-hobbled horses were grazing nearby. Evidently, Ensor did not believe in paying stabling fees if they could be avoided. Moving silently, he made a half-circle around the wagon and approached from the dark side. There was a saddle horse in the deeper shadows, tethered to a wagon wheel, and Kendrick eased his gun out of leather. Then he saw a figure seated by the dying camp-fire. Unable to make out details, he stepped around the end of the wagon, cocking his gun as he did so.

The man by the fire heard the metallic clicks of the gun being cocked and hurled himself to one side.

'Hold it,' Kendrick rapped, 'or I'll kill you.'

The man stopped instantly and raised his hands.

'I can't see a damn thing in this light,' Kendrick observed. 'Who are you?'

'Buster Fenton,' came the growled reply, and Kendrick grinned.

'On your feet, Buster,' he rasped, 'and keep your hands clear of your belt. You figured to have an early night, huh?'

'Something like that.' Fenton arose and lifted his hands shoulder-high. 'I don't wanta tangle with you, Deputy.'

'That's fine.' Kendrick spoke with a confidence he was far from feeling. He went in close, snaked Fenton's pistol from its holster, and did not forget the man's knife. He tossed the weapons away into the shadows. 'I want to talk with you. I didn't like the look of the man you were with earlier — the sharp-faced one wearing two guns — so I followed you around town. I saw you go into the law office and confront Hamley. It sure surprised me when Hamley let you hold sway over him, and I liked when you drew your gun and stuck the muzzle on his nose. He didn't bat an eyelid. But I didn't hear what was being said, so tell me about it.'

Fenton cursed fitfully.

'You sure got a long nose, Deputy. But I don't remember doing what you say you saw. Mebbe you were tailing some other guy. I don't like Hamley, and wouldn't go into his law office to save my life. Ask him about it.'

Kendrick slid his left foot forward a half-pace and unleashed the bunched knuckles of his left hand in a powerful hook that crashed against Fenton's chin. Fenton uttered a cry and fell backwards, his shoulders landing in the dying embers of the fire. Cursing, he rolled clear and surged to his feet. As he straightened, the muzzle of Kendrick's ready gun jabbed into his stomach, halting him abruptly.

'Don't get smart with me,' Kendrick rapped. 'Hamley's dead. I killed him about five minutes ago. So wise up, mister, or you'll join that crooked deputy in the undertaker's parlour.'

'Hamley's dead? Jeez! There'll be hell to pay for this. I wouldn't wanta be in your boots, nohow, Deputy. Hamley had powerful friends, and they'll want a reckoning with you when they hear about this.'

'What friends?' Kendrick seized hold of Fenton's shirt front and twisted, pulling the man close, at the same time jabbing the gun muzzle into his belly. 'Give me some names. I wanta know what's goin' on around here.'

Kendrick sensed Fenton's sudden attempt at resistance. The man's right shoulder lifted slightly and there was a shifting of weight from one foot to the other. Kendrick smashed his head forward in a vicious butt, and although his hatbrim took some of the power out of the blow it was sufficient to set Fenton back on his heels. Kendrick maintained his hold on the man's shirt. Fenton sagged in his grip. Kendrick shook him, supporting his weight.

'This could go on all night,' Kendrick said harshly. 'Open up, Fenton. I want some answers, and you're gonna give them to me no matter what persuasion I have to use.'

He caught the sound of boots on the hard ground at his back and whirled, swinging Fenton around to place the man between himself and the approaching newcomer.

'Is that you, Buster?' Al Ensor demanded as he came up. 'Things are happening in town. I saw Jenny with Arch Kington, and spotted you with Wiley. Did you get Hamley to throw in with you? He sure is a nuisance, blowing hot and cold over the deal ever since it was set up. How was he thinking tonight? Is he in with us?'

Then Ensor realized that Fenton was not alone, and his right hand darted to the butt of his gun.

'You couldn't be that stupid!' Kendrick said sharply. 'Leave it be or you're dead, Ensor.'

The pedlar froze, recognizing Kendrick's voice. 'What's going on here?' he demanded. 'What have you done now, Buster?'

'Get rid of your gun,' Kendrick ordered. 'Then we'll talk.'

'You can't treat me like this,' Ensor protested. 'You're picking on me every time you see me. I'll have a word with Lorimer about it.'

'You'll be seeing him a lot quicker than you think,' Kendrick retorted. 'I won't tell you again. Get rid of your gun.'

Ensor disarmed himself, grumbling. Kendrick thrust Fenton forward to join Ensor.

'Head for the jail,' he ordered, 'and don't try to escape.'

'I don't want to escape,' Fenton snarled. 'I wanta be around when the boys turn up to deal with you.'

'Keep talking,' Kendrick told him as they headed for the back of the livery barn. 'What boys are you talking about?'

'Keep your mouth shut, you fool!' Ensor rapped. 'Can't you see what his game is? He's digging for details. He doesn't know a blamed thing, so leave it that way.'

They passed through the stable and went along the street to the law office. Pete Sanchez, the undertaker, was bringing Hamley's body out of the office when they arrived, supervising two helpers who struggled to get the big cadaver through the close confines of the doorway. Ensor cursed as he looked at the dead man.

'Yeah,' Kendrick observed. 'Take a good look at him. I reckon his death is due to your business, whatever it is you're up to. Get inside the office and we'll start unravelling your movements. I want a full statement from both of you, and you better come across with the truth.'

There were several townsmen in the office, looking at the bullet hole in the desk, sniffing at the gunsmoke permeating the air, and all talking at once. They fell silent when Fenton and Ensor entered, followed closely by Kendrick, and stood gazing at the two prisoners as if they had never seen either man before.

'If you've got no business with the law right now then get outa here,' Kendrick said curtly. 'I'm real busy.'

'Are those two under arrest, Chuck?' Tom Mullin, the town storekeeper and mayor, was tall and thin, his narrow shoulders hunched, his face badly weathered. His dark eyes bored into Kendrick.

'Yeah. I've pulled them in for questioning. Have you got someone who'll take care of the jail until Lorimer can send another deputy?'

'Who killed Hamley?' Mullin persisted, pushing back his shoulders and assuming his official voice. 'The rumour is that you plugged him.'

Kendrick nodded. 'Hamley drew on me, so I had no choice. It was him or me. Now get out of here, all of you. I got work to do.'

He stood watching his prisoners, pistol covering them, until the townsmen had departed. Mullin was the last to go, and he paused by the street door.

'Jed Armstrong usually stands in as jailer when he's needed,' he said. 'I'll send him over.'

'Thanks.' Kendrick motioned to a bunch of keys lying on the desk. 'Pick them up and lead the way through to the cells, Ensor,' he said curtly. 'Let's get this business settled. I don't plan to be stuck in here all night.'

'And me neither!' Ensor rapped. 'You got nothing on me. You can't throw me in jail.' He glared fiercely at Kendrick, but quailed before the deputy's hard gaze and picked up the cell keys. Shrugging, he led the way into the cell block, where a couple of lamps shone dimly, and unlocked a cell door.

'Inside,' Kendrick ordered. He thrust Fenton forward into the cell behind Ensor and slammed the metal door, turning the key in the lock and removing it. 'I'm gonna leave you two to sweat for a spell, and when I come back I'll wanta know what's been going on around here.'

He looked around then, and saw that the other cells were empty. He had put Wiley into a cell earlier, and now the gunman was gone. Hamley must have turned him loose. He walked to the door and paused to enable either prisoner to break down and talk. But neither had anything to say, and Kendrick went back into the office. He dropped a hand to his gun when he saw Jenny Ensor standing in the office just inside the street door. His keen gaze narrowed as he took in her appearance.

'What's going on?' she demanded. 'I heard that you've arrested Dad and

Buster.' She came forward to confront him, and he caught the tang of cheap perfume clinging to her dress. 'You can't keep them in jail, Deputy. Why have you locked them up?'

'I'll do a deal with you,' he replied. 'Tell me the truth about what they were up to this evening and I'll consider turning them loose.'

'What do you mean? What could they have been doing that's against the law? Dad said he was gonna have a drink or two and renew acquaintance with some of his previous customers. He is running a business, you know.'

'What about you?' he countered. 'What were you doing with the cattle-buyer? I thought you were planning to get hitched to Fenton, so why were you out with another man?'

'You've been watching my movements!' Her lips tightened ominously as she gazed at him. 'Is that all you've got to do? The county is going to the dogs, and you're wasting your time watching me. That's an unhealthy way to spend your life, Deputy.'

'You're talking a lot but you ain't saying anything,' he observed. 'If you want to get your pa outa jail then you'll have to come clean. Tell me what's going on. What is Al mixed up in?'

She shook her head. 'You're talking riddles. What's really on your mind?'

Kendrick suppressed a sigh. He realized that his undercover job had blown up in his face. He could not go on tracking these people because they would be watching for him after this evening.

'All right,' he said heavily. 'I'll lay it on the line. Listen to the questions I have buzzing around in my head, and if you can give me clear answers to them then Al will walk outa here in minutes.'

'I'm listening,' she said thinly.

'I've been following your wagon since it left Clearwater Creek. I trailed Fenton when he rode out, and also the three riders who showed up at your camp in the middle of the night. I guessed they were outlaws, and that was proved when they got themselves killed in a shoot-out at the trading post back along the trail. So who were those three?'

'They weren't outlaws. As far as I knew, they were cowpokes on their way back from Abilene. They trailed a herd north for the XL, so they said. Did you kill them?'

'Nope. I was watching their movements.' Kendrick explained what had happened at the trading post. 'They sure didn't act like cowpokes. But let's leave that for a moment, huh? You and Fenton are gonna be wed. Ain't that so?'

'I ain't agreed to no such thing.' Her expression changed and she clenched her hands. 'Buster has got big ideas, and I don't figure in them nohow. Anyway, I wouldn't marry him if he paid me.'

'So what were you doing with Arch Kington? Is he a cattle-buyer?

'That's what he says. If you don't believe it then ask him. He talks cattle all the time, and reckons there's more profit in buying stock here in Texas and trailing them north himself than waiting for the herds to be trailed up to him.'

'So why were you out with him, all dolled up and looking fit to kill? You got no interest in the cattle business.'

'It ain't the business I'm interested in but the man. Arch has got money coming out of his ears, and I'm tired of traipsing around with Pa and that wagon of his. I aim to marry a rich man, live the good life, and Arch is the best prospect I've seen in a long time.' She paused, glaring at him. 'Is there something wrong with that? I suppose you've got a law against it.'

'You got an answer for everything, but you still ain't getting to the point,' Kendrick said. 'And I'm wasting time, so I'm gonna throw you in jail to give you time to think over your position. Come the morning, you should know what you've got to do. If you stand out against the law then you'll have a good life, I don't think. Come on, you can share a cell with your pa.'

'Wait!' A note of desperation sounded in her voice. 'I can't afford to be locked up right now. Trust me just a little and I promise I'll talk to you in the morning. Let me go now and I'll check up on one or two points I must admit are bothering me, and if something bad is going on then I'll tell you about it.'

He shook his head. 'I can't trust you after the way you've acted. Remember what happened back in Clearwater Creek? You damn near split my skull in two and it still hurts. What were you and Fenton doing there, anyway? He was threatening you with his knife when I set on eyes on you, but you covered up for him and then busted my head. That ain't the reaction I would expect from someone who is innocent, so don't blame me for doubting you.'

'I was desperate then, and acted on the spur of the moment.' She spoke slowly. 'I'm sorry for what I did, but I could only think of saving my father. I thought he was in bad trouble when I left him at the creek and rode into town to talk to the sheriff — that's how desperate I was — but Buster headed me off, and you came upon us as he was trying to persuade me to go back to camp.'

'So what kind of trouble did you think your father was in? He leads a simple life, selling pots and pans. Unless' — Kendrick's tone hardened — 'he's using that as a cover to hide his real purpose in life.'

'You've got a nasty, suspicious mind,' she declared, gazing at him with narrowed eyes, her face expressing a whole range of fleeting emotions. Then she covered her eyes with her hands and burst into tears. Kendrick gazed at her impassively, believing that she was trying to fool him. He grasped her shoulder, led her to the desk, and eased her into a seat. Then he sat and waited for her to recover her composure. The silence deepened, and when at last she looked up, her eyes were filled with shimmering tears.

'You're a hard man,' she accused. 'Doesn't anything move you?'

'I want to help you,' he responded, 'but I can only do that if you tell me the truth. I do know a little of what's going on, and enough to know when you are holding back or lying. If you didn't know what is happening, and have just begun to suspect it, then the best thing you can do is tell me your suspicions. Then I'll help you however I can. But if you hold out against me then you can only make matters worse for yourself and your father.'

'What do you suspect my pa of doing?'

'Passing on information to outlaws.'

'What outlaws? Pa wouldn't know an outlaw if he saw one. And what is the information he's supposed to be passing on?'

'Someone is learning about the banks in various towns around the county and passing the information on to Blink Darra and his bunch. Sheriff Lorimer is a cagey old lawman, and he's worked out that soon after your pa passes through a town it is robbed by the gang. It's more than coincidence, so don't bother denying it.'

'And am I supposed to be in on this too?' she demanded.

'I wouldn't know about that.' Kendrick shook his head. 'All I know is that I got orders to watch your movements, and what I've seen so far inclines me to believe that Lorimer has got it right. Fenton has been meeting up with hardcases. Outlaws have dropped by your camp in the night to talk with your pa, and you're tangled up with a cattle-buyer in a county where there's wholesale rustling going on.'

'Are you calling Arch Kington a thief?'

'Cut it out,' he said roughly. 'I'll know the rights of that soon enough, you can bet.'

He broke off as the street door was opened and a man entered the office. Tall and well built, he looked to be in his middle thirties. He was wearing a holstered pistol on his right thigh, and smiled as he came towards the desk.

'Howdy,' he greeted. 'I'm Jed Armstrong. Tom Mullin said you need a jailer. I usually stand in for the law when they're short-handed. Have we got any prisoners?'

'Howdy, Jed.' Kendrick nodded. 'I got Al Ensor and Buster Fenton behind bars. I'm gonna question them in the morning. This is Jenny Ensor.'

'Yeah.' Armstrong nodded. 'I know Miss Ensor by sight. What's Al been up to? I've known him for years, and he ain't the type to tangle with the law.'

'I aim to find out what he's been doing,' Kendrick replied.

'And Miss Ensor? Is she under arrest?'

'No.' Kendrick reached a decision. 'I got no reason to hold her. She wants to see her pa.' He saw relief shining in her eyes. 'You can see him now, and then I'll walk you to the hotel. You'd better stay there tonight. It won't be safe, you being alone in that wagon.'

'Don't worry about me,' she responded. 'I can take care of myself.'

'I don't doubt that for a minute.' Kendrick removed his hat and rubbed his skull.

He escorted Jenny into the cell block and stood by while she spoke with her father. Al Ensor stood inside the cell, gripping the bars, plainly ill at ease. Fenton was stretched out on a bunk, evidently asleep.

'You got to get me outa here, Jenny,' Ensor said. 'I can't stand being locked up.'

'You can walk outa here now, if you tell me what's been going on and who you are mixed up with,' Kendrick told him. 'Spill the beans and save me a lot of trouble, and if you ain't too involved in the crookedness then you won't have much to worry about, but keep clammed up and you'll see the inside of the state prison before you're done.'

Ensor looked at him with despair in his gaze, shaking his head slowly.

'I ain't never done a bad thing in my

life,' he said. 'You gotta believe that.'

'It ain't for me to make the decisions,' Kendrick said. 'I got my orders, and that's all I need to know. If you got anything you want Jenny to do then tell her now and she can see to it first thing in the morning.'

'There's a lawyer got an office along the street,' Ensor said, his tone suddenly brisk. 'Go see him, Jenny. Tell him about this and he'll have me out of here come morning, you see if he don't.'

'That'll do now,' Kendrick said. 'Let's go, Jenny. I'll take you along the street. I feel kind of responsible for you under the circumstances.'

The girl flashed him a look that was filled with hatred, but she turned away instantly and Kendrick escorted her back into the office. Armstrong was now seated behind the desk, and he grinned.

'You can leave me to it,' he said. 'I know the routine.'

Kendrick nodded and crossed to the

street door. He opened it and stepped aside for Jenny to precede him, and the next instant the night was filled with gun thunder and flying lead. Orange flashes winked and died as he hurled himself to the floor, and hot lead crackled around him as he reached out a long arm to the girl and dragged her out of the line of fire.

6

Kendrick drew his gun and prepared to fight but Jenny grasped his arm and clung to him with all her strength. He tried to shake her off as the first volley of shots died away, and paused when a harsh voice on the street yelled in an echoing tone:

'Hey, you in the office. Come on out with your hands up or we'll come in and get you.'

'Armstrong, for God's sake douse that lamp,' Kendrick rapped as he grasped Jenny's shoulder and thrust her out of his way. 'Stay down and keep quiet,' he growled as Armstrong plunged the office into darkness.

'Don't be a fool,' she responded. 'If you stick your nose outside, they'll kill you.'

'What do you know about them? Are they your pa's friends?'

125

'It doesn't matter who they are.' Her tone was steady but filled with tension, and she clutched at his arm. 'Do you want to get yourself killed?'

'I've got a job to do, and nothing will stand in the way of that.' Kendrick started to rise but Jenny clung to him.

'What's it gonna be?' demanded the voice outside. 'Are you coming out?'

'What's going on?' Jed Armstrong called from the back of the office. 'Who are those men out there?'

'Your guess is as good as mine,' Kendrick retorted. 'Come and hold Jenny. Keep her out of my way.'

She tried to get away from him then, but Kendrick held her until Armstrong came and took hold of her. Kendrick sighed with relief and got to his feet. He stood to one side of the door and peered out into the street. A gun flashed immediately from the darkness and a bullet splintered the door-jamb close to his face. He ducked away instinctively, a mild curse spilling from his taut lips.

'Time's up,' the voice outside informed him in a strident tone. 'You ain't coming out so we're coming in.'

Several guns began shooting, and bullets slammed into the front wall of the office. Kendrick dropped to one knee. Lifting his gun, he aimed at a gun flash and fired, then began shooting rapidly, shifting his aim to cover the flashes that tattered the dark shadows around the street. He estimated that half a dozen guns were shooting at him. His ears were deafened by gunfire. Then his hammer clicked on an empty cartridge and he hastily reloaded. The shooting ceased abruptly, and Kendrick grinned despite his tension. Whoever they were, the men outside were realizing that they had not selected an easy chore. He strained to pick up noise, but his ears were ringing from the crash of the rapid detonations. He eased forward slightly to get a glimpse of the street, ready to flatten out at the first return to shooting and, unable to see anything in the darkness, awaited developments while gun echoes faded into an uneasy silence.

'Someone's trying to get in through the back door,' Armstrong warned from the back of the office.

Kendrick heard heavy battering sounds as the rear of the jail was attacked.

'Take Jenny with you and watch the back door,' he instructed. 'Don't shoot unless they look like breaking in.'

Armstrong moved away, taking Jenny with him, and Kendrick returned his attention to the street. A gun crashed from across the thoroughfare and a bullet plucked at the brim of his Stetson. He returned fire instantly, before the reddish flash died away, and the shadows opposite moved slightly as a man lurched forward half a pace and then crumpled to the ground. Kendrick nodded. This was more like it.

A gun crackled furiously from Kendrick's left and the big front window shattered. Kendrick ducked, and when he straightened a lamp that had been hanging on an awning post just outside was sailing in through the broken window. It bounced on the floor, its glass shattering, and burning fuel spread across the office. Voracious flames licked hungrily at the dry woodwork. He fired at a shadowy figure outside the window, and heard a hoarse cry as the man collected a slug for his trouble.

The tempo of shooting rose quickly, compelling Kendrick to move back from the doorway. Slugs snarled into the office and crackled around him. He dropped to one knee, holding his fire but covering the broken window and the open door. A man stuck his hand around the door-jamb and emptied a pistol indiscriminately into the office. Kendrick fired and the pistol went flying. The shattered hand was withdrawn. But almost immediately two men lunged in through the doorway, coming from either side, and Kendrick snapped off two quick shots without pausing to aim. Both men crumpled instantly, their guns thudding heavily on the floor as they fell inertly on the threshold.

The shooting dwindled away then, and Kendrick reloaded his pistol. Gunsmoke was thick in his nostrils. He suddenly felt a need of fresh air, and approached the door cautiously. Gun in hand, he bent to check the two men lying in the doorway, and grunted when he discovered that both were dead. He kept low and risked a look outside, ready to duck, but nothing happened and he gazed around, his eyes squinted to pierce the shadows. He saw two men lying motionless in the street and another opposite on the far side. Two dark figures were running away along the street and he resisted the impulse to shoot at them.

He exhaled slowly, sensing that the immediate danger was over. The men, whoever they were, had pulled out. He straightened and stepped out of the office, pushing his back against the front wall while he checked out his surroundings. He saw the two figures in the distance to the left entering the saloon.

Sticking his head inside the office, he called for the jailer. Armstrong emerged from the cell block, still holding Jenny by the arm.

'It looks like they've gone,' he said. 'Cover me while I bring in the bodies. I need to know who was shooting at us.'

'Shall I lock Miss Ensor in a cell?' Armstrong demanded. 'Holding on to her is cramping my movements. She keeps trying to break away.'

'Yeah. Put her in a cell. She'll keep until later.'

'I thought you weren't going to lock me up tonight,' Jenny said angrily.

'That was before the shooting started,' Kendrick observed. 'If a bunch of men were prepared to die to get you and your pa out of jail then I'd be a fool to turn you loose.'

He waited while Armstrong took Jenny back into the cell block, and grinned fleetingly when he heard the clash of a metal door being closed and

131

the metallic clinking of cell keys.

'I feel easier now,' Armstrong said when he returned. 'That girl is three parts wildcat.'

Kendrick rubbed his head where Jenny had hit him in Clearwater Creek and mentally agreed. He checked his gun before stepping outside once more.

'These two are dead,' he remarked. 'Just keep your eyes open while I move around outside. There are three or four bodies I want to bring in.'

He went unhesitatingly into the open, holstered his gun and grasped two of the men by the scruffs of their necks. Without pausing, he dragged them into the office. As he turned to go outside again he heard the sound of voices in the adjacent shadows and drew his gun.

'Who's out there?' he demanded.

'Doc McKee and Mayor Mullin,' came the reply.

'Come on in,' Kendrick invited, and the two men appeared in the doorway.

'We had to wait until the shooting was over before we could approach,'

Mullin said with a degree of apology in his voice. 'There was no telling what was happening. We didn't know who was shooting at whom.'

'I still don't know who started it,' Kendrick said, 'but I sure as hell mean to find out. Did you see anyone leaving this area after the shooting?'

'A couple of men passed us and went into Delaney's saloon,' McKee volunteered. 'I got a good look at one of them. He was one of those trail hands who came into town with the cattle-buyer.'

'Let's have some light in here now so we can see what we've got.' Kendrick stamped on the floor where the tiny flames being fed by the last of the fuel from the lamp were dying out. Armstrong fetched a lamp from the cells, and Kendrick looked around at the grim scene now revealed. He checked the inert figures on the floor. One of them was Wiley, whom Fenton had set to watch Kendrick, and Hamley had turned Wiley loose after Kendrick jailed him. So that tied Fenton in with the gun attack on the jail.

'Can you put names to any of these men?' he asked. He toed Wiley with a dusty boot. 'I know this one. He was prowling around with Fenton earlier.'

'I've seen them around town, but I don't know who they are,' Mullin said. 'I'm certain they came in with that cattle buyer, Kington. There is about a dozen of them, all told, and they've been going around the town as if they owned it. You know what trail hands are.'

Kendrick nodded. 'Is there someone reliable enough in town who would ride to Clearwater Creek and carry a report of this shooting to the sheriff?' he asked.

'Yep.' Mullin nodded. 'I'll send Tom Yates to you. He can be trusted. Write down what you want Lorimer to know and Tom will be here in ten minutes to collect it. He works for me in the store, so I know he's reliable.'

Mullin went to the door, eager to

help, and the doctor accompanied him.

'Can we get that window boarded up tonight?' Kendrick asked.

'I'm the town carpenter,' Armstrong said. 'Do you want me to take care of it? I'll do a temporary job. It won't take long.'

Kendrick nodded. 'Give me the cell keys while you're out of the office.' He held out his hand for them, then went through to the cells, where a single lamp gave barely enough light to see by.

'Fenton, what was your connection with Wiley?' he asked. 'You two seemed to know each other real well.'

'I don't know who you mean,' Fenton replied. 'I never knew anyone named Wiley.'

'Don't start that again. You know who I'm talking about. You were with him in the saloon, and set him to watch my movements.'

'Not me. I don't know who you mean,' Fenton replied doggedly.

'You do,' Kendrick insisted quietly.

'No. I don't know who you mean,'

Fenton persisted, 'but what about him?'

'He's lying dead on the floor of the office. He was one of those men doing the shooting. They were fixing to bust you and Al out of here. But they badly underestimated the law, meaning me. I reckon they thought they were coming up against Hamley, huh? The way you were acting towards Hamley earlier, I'd say you had a good hold on him.'

There was a shocked silence at Kendrick's words. Neither Fenton nor Ensor would meet his gaze. He waited several moments, but it was obvious that they had no wish to say anything. He looked at Jenny's taut, frightened face, but could find no pity in his heart for her, believing that she was as deeply involved in what was going on as either man.

'It's fine by me if you don't want to set me straight on what's happening,' he said, turning away. 'We can continue this in the morning.'

He left the cell block, hesitating in the hope that one of them would call him back to reveal what he wanted to know, but neither man spoke, and he closed the connecting door and locked it before turning to find Pete Sanchez, the undertaker, standing in the office waiting to talk to him.

'Get those bodies out of here, and let me have their details in the morning,' Kendrick said. 'I don't know any of them, so ask around for names.'

'There's another man lying dead on the street,' Sanchez told him. 'Looks like he crawled away before he died.'

'Let's take a look at him.' Kendrick suppressed a sigh. He followed the undertaker out to the street and looked at the body stretched out under a lantern hanging from a nearby post. He shook his head. 'I don't know anything about this one either,' he said. 'I suppose he was mixed up in the shooting. Looks like a bullet finished him. Put him with the others, and get all the bodies identified.'

Sanchez nodded. 'I hope there won't be any more of this for a spell,' he said.

'I'm gonna be rushed off my feet as it is. Have you got any idea what's going on?'

'None at all, but I'm sure gonna find out.' Kendrick dropped a hand to his gun as footsteps sounded in the shadows. He turned to see a tall figure approaching, and recognized Arch Kington, the cattle-buyer. 'You've saved me the trouble of looking you up, Kington,' he greeted. 'Come into the office. I got some of your men inside, and I need you to tell me about them.'

He kept his hand on his gun butt as they entered the office, and saw Kington's shock as the man laid his eyes on the dead men. The cattle-buyer gasped and shook his head.

'What on earth happened?' he demanded. 'How did they get shot?'

'They attacked this office.' Kendrick spoke harshly, his tone resolute. 'Were they acting on your orders?'

'My orders?' A trace of anger sounded in Kington's hoarse voice. 'Why would I want an attack made on the jail?'

'To free Ensor and Fenton. They're the only prisoners.' Kendrick watched the cattle-buyer closely. Kington seemed genuinely shocked by the grim sight. His face was pale and he looked sick, but his eyes were shrewd, filled with calculation, and his tone was firm when he spoke.

'I don't understand.' Kington shook his head. 'I don't know Ensor or Fenton.'

'You spent the evening with Ensor's daughter, Jenny, and when I saw the two of you together you seemed to be old friends. If you don't know either man then how did you meet Jenny? She saw no one from town before she arrived, yet the minute she got here she put on a dress and hurried to meet you. Someone must have seen her on the trail before she got to town and mentioned that you were here.'

'That's preposterous!' Kington shook his head. 'Where is Jenny? Didn't she tell you that we met in the hotel?'

'She's not saying anything yet,'

Kendrick said sharply. 'But she will spill the beans before I get through with her. Have you got a gun on you?'

Kington stared at him defiantly. 'What's it to you?' he demanded.

'Hand it over. I'm arresting you. I'm gonna hold you until I've investigated this business. You brought these men from Kansas so you're responsible for them, and I can only assume that they were acting on your orders. All of them were strangers here, and they had no reason to attack the jail unless someone ordered them to do so.'

'You can't arrest me on such flimsy evidence,' Kington snapped.

'Who's gonna stop me?' Kendrick grinned. 'Are you thinking that I'm the same kind of lawman Hamley was? Give me your gun, and be careful how you do it or you'll wind up dead on the floor with the rest of your bunch.' He drew his gun with a slick movement and covered Kington, who flinched, then instinctively raised his hands. 'Your gun,' he repeated, and the cattle-buyer produced a .38 pistol that was nestling in a holster in his left armpit.

'Through that door,' Kendrick ordered. 'That's the way to the cells. You've got the rest of the night to think this over, and then I'll expect a statement that will clear it up.'

'I don't know a thing about it,' Kington protested. 'You're making a big mistake.'

'I'll worry about that.' Kendrick followed the cattle-buyer into the cell block and unlocked a door. Kington entered the cell and Kendrick slammed the door and locked it. 'All friends together, huh?' he demanded, glancing at Ensor and Fenton as he departed. 'See you men tomorrow.'

He went back to the office to write a report for Lorimer, and was finishing it when a man entered the office. Kendrick dropped a hand to his gun.

'I'm Tom Yates,' the newcomer said. 'Mr Mullin told me to ride to Clearwater Creek with a report for

Sheriff Lorimer.'

'I've just finished it.' Kendrick handed over an envelope. 'Put this into the sheriff's hands. Don't give it to anyone else. I expect Lorimer will send a reply so wait for it. I need some fresh orders, and I'll stay here doing Hamley's job until you get back.'

'That'll be some time tomorrow afternoon,' Yates said.

Kendrick nodded. 'Fine. It'll give me time to look around and see what I can make of this trouble.'

'I think the cattle-buyer's trail hands are to blame for it all,' Yates said. 'They're a tough bunch, little better than trail scum. They've been annoying the womenfolk around town and scaring hell out of the men. Some of them came into the store, where I work, and lifted stock without paying for it. When I braced their trail boss, Pearson, he gave me some guff about asking Kington, the cattle-buyer, for the money.'

'I've met Pearson.' Kendrick nodded.

'He was pestering Jenny Ensor in the café earlier, and she was with Kington at the time. Kington didn't look too happy about the situation, but he took it without a word. Not the way I would expect an employer to act around his trail crew.'

'I'll hit the trail now.' Yates tucked the envelope inside his shirt and departed.

Jed Armstrong returned accompanied by another man. They were carrying lengths of timber, and Armstrong had a toolbox. Kendrick nodded when the two men set to work boarding up the broken window. He handed the office keys to Armstrong.

'I'm gonna take a stroll around the town,' he said. 'There are some loose ends I need to tie up before morning. Just keep an eye lifting for trouble, although I don't expect another attack on the jail.'

'It's quiet out there now,' Armstrong observed.

Kendrick drew his pistol and checked the loads. Leaving the office, he went to the saloon, keeping to the dense shadows, and stepped into an alley beside the saloon to peer into the building through a side window. His eyes glinted when he saw Pearson seated at a gaming-table with another apparent trail hand, for it was obvious to him that if Kington deserved to be in jail, then so did the men in Kington's employ. He let his gaze rove around the saloon, and spotted another trail hand standing at the bar just inside the batwings. He nodded. It looked as if Pearson was prepared for the arrival of the local law.

He turned and walked along the alley to the rear of the saloon. He stood in the darkness for some moments, trying to pierce the shadows with his sharp gaze. Then he found the back door to the building and, discovering that it was locked, put his foot into it, forcing it open. He stepped into a storeroom and opened an inner door.

He made his way to the door giving access to the bar and peered into the big room. Drawing his pistol, he went in to stand behind Pearson, keeping the man between himself and the trail hand seated opposite at the table. The man caught Kendrick's movement, glanced up, and froze at the sight of Kendrick's drawn gun. Pearson noted his companion's manner and half-turned until he could see Kendrick. His expression did not change, but he sat motionless.

'You got some sense,' Kendrick observed. He could see the trail hand down by the batwings. The man was watching the front door, and missed the play at the rear of the saloon. 'Both of you, keep your hands on the table.' He snaked Pearson's gun out of its holster and sniffed at the muzzle. 'This has been fired recently, which ties you in with the attack made on the jail.' He stuck the gun into his waistband and stepped around the table, lifting the second man's gun and checking it. 'Likewise this one. You both tried to force your way into the law office so I'm gonna do you a favour. I'll take you there now, and throw you in a cell.'

'You'd better talk to Arch Kington before you do anything stupid,' said Pearson.

'You can talk to him yourself.' Kendrick smiled. 'He's already in jail.'

The trail hand near the batwings suddenly looked in their direction, and Kendrick, with one eye on the man, saw him stiffen and reach for his holstered gun. The few townsmen in the saloon moved quickly out of the line of fire. Kendrick fired a shot as the trail hand's gun came up into the aim, and a raucous clap of gunfire shook the big room as the weapon recoiled against the heel of his hand. The man jerked under the impact of the slug that took him in the chest, then fell against the bar, his gun spilling from his hand. He slid to the floor and lay motionless.

Kendrick waited until the echoes of the shot faded, and, when full silence returned, he stepped backwards, waggling his deadly gun.

'On your feet,' he rapped. 'You know

where the jail is so head for it, and pick up your sidekick when you reach him.'

Pearson cursed as he got to his feet, but the deadly threat of Kendrick's gun gave him no alternative but to obey. His companion arose, and they walked to the batwings, their spurs jangling. The trail hand on the floor was unconscious, a patch of blood on his shirt front.

'Pick him up,' Kendrick ordered. 'He ain't dead. We'll get the doc to look at him soon as you're behind bars.'

Pearson glared at Kendrick but did as he was ordered. The wounded man was picked up and carried out to the street. Kendrick followed closely, his gun ready in his hand, and half a dozen townsmen followed him as they went along the street, intent on witnessing the finale of the situation.

Jed Armstrong looked up in surprise when Pearson and his companions entered the office. He saw Kendrick behind them and grinned.

'Nearly finished here,' he remarked. 'You've been doing some cleaning up of your own, huh?'

'I've about finished for the evening,' Kendrick said. 'These men will keep until morning.' He turned to a townsman, who was peering into the office from the street doorway. 'Go fetch Doc McKee. It's possible that he didn't hear the shot. Tell him I need him here as soon as he can make it.'

The man departed at a run. Kendrick motioned for Pearson and his companion to take the wounded man into the cell block, and followed closely. He locked all three in a cell, and grinned as he looked around at the taut faces peering at him from behind bars. Al Ensor was watching him, his face showing uneasiness, and Jenny looked uncomfortable, sitting on the foot of the bunk where Buster Fenton was stretched out trying to sleep.

'Looks like I got a full house,' Kendrick remarked. 'You can settle down for the night now. I don't plan on bringing in anyone else before tomorrow.'

Jenny arose quickly and came to the door of the cell, pushing her father aside.

'I can't stay in here all night,' she protested, her voice tremulous with anger. 'You wanted me to tell you things. All right, I'll do it. Anything to get me out of here.'

'Jenny, you better stay right where you are,' Cal Pearson said harshly. 'Open your mouth and you won't live to see tomorrow.'

'Cut that out,' Kendrick rapped. He unlocked the door of the cell where Jenny was standing and motioned for her to step out. She did so, sighing heavily, and Kendrick slammed the door and locked it.

'I'm warning you, Jenny,' Pearson growled. 'You tell him anything about our business and you're done for.'

Kendrick put a hand on Jenny's shoulder and pushed her gently towards the office. He was keen to talk to her now, sensing that she was inclined to make disclosures. As she seated herself beside the desk in the office the street door opened and Doc McKee entered, carrying a leather medical bag. Armstrong was putting the finishing touches to boarding up the broken window.

'Keep an eye on Jenny, Jed,' Kendrick said. 'She's not to leave the office.'

He took the doctor through to the cells and stood by while the wounded trail hand was examined. McKee applied a bandage to the wound and emerged from the cell.

'He'll keep until morning,' he said. 'It's not serious. The bullet never touched a bone. I'll drop by tomorrow.'

Kendrick saw the doctor out before turning his attention to Jenny Ensor, who was sitting dejectedly on the chair by the desk. The girl's expression revealed the true extent of her feelings, and Kendrick experienced a faint hope of making a breakthrough in the situation that existed here in Red Mesa. He needed something to break the impasse before the sheriff arrived on the morrow, something that would enable him to clean up on the lawless element in the town, and for the first time since meeting Jenny, he fancied that the girl was now at a disadvantage and ready to reveal what she knew.

7

Jed Armstrong went back to finishing the broken front window when Kendrick sat down behind the desk and looked into Jenny's eyes. She was reluctant to meet his gaze, and he reached across the desk and grasped her left wrist. She tried to pull away but he held her firmly and she finally looked at him.

'This won't work if you're not prepared to tell me the whole truth,' he said. 'I can't settle for less than that, and it will be better if you talk to me now rather than to the sheriff tomorrow. You were in Clearwater Creek the other day to tell Lorimer something, so what's changed since then?'

'I'm so worried about my father,' she said hesitatingly. 'He's caught in a situation that's getting worse every day.'

'Then tell me about it.' There was no

trace of eagerness in Kendrick's tone. 'I've said I'll help where I can, so what's the problem?'

'They'll kill my father if word gets out.' She shook her head. 'I don't think I can take that risk.'

'Let me tell you what I think the situation is from what I've seen since I arrived in Red Mesa.' Kendrick considered for a moment, marshalling his thoughts. 'Arch Kington sent in a gang of rustlers to clean out the range. The stolen cattle are being held somewhere near here, and Kington has arrived with Pearson and a trail crew to get the stock moved north. Is that right?'

Jenny nodded slowly. 'Partly,' she admitted, and sighed heavily.

'Where does your pa come into it?'

'He doesn't at all.'

'So what's the deal? You rode into Clearwater Creek to see the sheriff because you were worried about your pa. What was so bad about it that Fenton was using a knife to scare you into changing your mind? That is what

153

he was doing, huh? And when I stepped in you hit me with a rifle butt.'

Again she nodded slowly, and Kendrick could see that she was trying to decide if she could trust him. He remained silent, studying her features, noting that her nose was turned up and her mouth seemed slightly too wide for her face. But her skin was clear and her blue eyes were appealing. He shook his head and suppressed a sigh.

'Give me something to work on,' he commanded. 'You won't get any help from the sheriff. He sees everything as black or white, and doesn't give a damn about motives or circumstances. If a man does something wrong then he's guilty, and that's the end of it as far as Lorimer is concerned. He won't give anyone an inch. I got the feeling your pa has edged himself into a corner and would like to get out but can't. Well, I'm prepared to help him if by doing so I can stop the rustlers and get a line on the Darra gang.'

Her eyes narrowed. 'What do you

know about Blink Darra and his bunch? They're mighty dangerous men — real killers.'

'I know that. Twelve years ago they killed my father in the street in Bitter Creek. He was the town marshal, and tried to stop the gang robbing the bank.'

'I saw that happen!' Her face paled and she clasped her hands together. 'I've had nightmares about it ever since. I was only a kid then, but your father was the bravest man that lived. He walked towards the gang, firing two pistols, until he was shot down. He was alone, and there were seven in the gang, but he killed four of them before they got him.'

Kendrick's face turned bleak at her words and his teeth clicked together as he fought down a wave of emotion. A sigh escaped him. He swallowed noisily and sucked in a deep breath. His eyes took on a dangerous glitter as he narrowed them and gazed at her.

'I heard an account of it,' he said

harshly. 'Did you see who fired the shot that killed him?'

She gazed at him, held by the power of his gaze. Shaking her head, she said, 'It is so long ago now, and I didn't know the names of the gang in those days.'

'I heard that Trig Weevil did it.' His voice tremored.

'I don't know. There was so much confusion. Men were shooting in all directions, horses were running around the street. Guns were banging and gunsmoke was thick. I was crouching in the wagon. I saw your father fall, and then hid my face until it was all over.'

'How did your father happen to be in Broken Ridge when the gang hit the bank?'

She shook her head. 'Just coincidence, I think. Pa must have visited every town in Texas over the last twenty years.'

'The sheriff says he has evidence that your pa is working for the gang, checking out banks and getting information about local conditions.'

'That's not true.'

'It's why I was sent to follow the wagon and watch your movements, and I must say that what I've seen makes me think the sheriff is right. There's something going on that's not right, not by a long rope, and if you don't come across with the truth then I'm gonna believe the accusations and act accordingly. Your pa could hang for his part in it.'

'It's not Pa doing it,' she said sharply. 'Buster Fenton is in Darra's gang, and he was sent along with us to check on the banks in the towns Pa visits. Pa just went about his business while Fenton pretended to be working with him, but all Fenton did was get the details Darra wanted. And before Fenton joined us another member of the gang did the same job. If Pa hadn't gone along with the idea, Darra would have killed him, and me. That was the hold Darra had over us.'

Kendrick studied her face, trying to gauge the degree of truth in what she was saying. She kept her eyes on his face, and he could not guess at the thoughts running through her mind.

'Do you know where the gang is hiding out?'

She shook her head. 'We never had anything to do with them. If we saw them on the trail we ignored them, unless they stopped for any information that Fenton had collected.'

'Like those three did the other night, huh? They got themselves killed at Stafford's trading post in a shoot-out with the Circle B outfit.' Satisfaction sounded in Kendrick's voice. 'Are you willing to give evidence against Fenton?'

'What will happen to my pa if I do?' she countered.

'I'm willing to take a chance on you. I'll turn your pa loose if you co-operate.'

'What do I have to do? If I spill the beans, the gang will be after Pa and me. They would kill us to shut us up.'

'I'll be looking up Darra and his bunch when I get a line on them,' Kendrick said. 'They won't give you any trouble if I can get them under my gun.'

'You haven't caught up with them over the years,' she responded. 'What makes you think you'll be lucky this time?'

'I've got Fenton in jail, for one thing. He might start talking when he finds out he's slated for the high jump.'

'The Darra gang has robbed banks in many of the towns through Texas. Fenton has talked about some of those jobs, including several he took part in before Darra pushed him on to us. Fenton is a killer. He bragged about killing the town marshal in Dogtown three years ago.'

'I remember that raid.' Kendrick nodded. 'The marshal at Dogtown, Frank Beamish, was a pard of my father's many years ago. So Fenton killed Beamish. Well, that'll do to hold him for now. Are you prepared to make a statement detailing what you've told me?'

'I will if you turn my father loose

now, and give us time to get out of this neck of the woods before anyone else is freed. Kington and his trail hands are handling the rustling. I can't prove that for you, but I know Kington operates under the protection of Blink Darra, so the outlaws must be getting a rake-off from the rustlers.'

'So that's how it's done.' Kendrick's mind flitted back over the acts of lawlessness that had occurred over the recent past, and several questions that had been bothering him now found answers. 'Look, I can't let you go yet,' he mused. 'The sheriff will want to question you, and what you've told me will have to be proved. But you'll be under the protection of the law, and when the badmen are convicted, you and your pa will be free to go.'

'Does that mean Pa will have to stay in jail until then?' She was clearly disappointed, and seemed to freeze out the friendliness that had crept into her voice.

'There won't be a safer place for him

at the moment. If I turned him loose now I should think word will get out and some gunnie will take care of him for the gang.'

'But you can't leave him locked in with Fenton,' she protested. 'Fenton is a real killer. Back in Clearwater Creek, just before you came on the scene, Fenton was threatening to slit my throat if I didn't go back to camp with him. I think he would have done it, too.'

Kendrick got to his feet. 'I'll fetch your pa in here. Let's hear what he's got to say about it.'

He went through to the cells, and the talking that was going on among the prisoners stopped instantly at his appearance. Hard eyes watched him as he unlocked the door of Ensor's cell. Ensor was standing. Buster Fenton was sprawled out on a bunk, his merciless gaze unblinking as he watched Kendrick, who motioned for Ensor to leave the cell. The pedlar emerged reluctantly and stood motionless while Kendrick relocked the cell door.

'If you know what's good for you you'll keep your mouth shut, Ensor,' Fenton growled.

Kendrick pushed Ensor in the back and the man walked through to the office. Jed Armstrong brought a chair to the desk and Ensor sat down beside his daughter. He looked at Jenny, his seamed face showing doubt, and he seemed to be aware of the situation for he grimaced.

'What have you done, Jenny?' he demanded. 'If you've told him anything then we're both good as dead.'

'I've only done what you should have years ago,' she declared. 'This has gone on too long. You've said many times that you wanted out of it. Well, I've taken the step now, and it will be all right.'

'All you have to do is give me the facts about your association with the outlaws,' Kendrick said. 'Make a voluntary statement, and if what you say tallies with what Jenny has told me then you can both be heading out of here tomorrow.'

Ensor shook his head. His eyes held a hunted expression. He glanced around the office as if wishing he was many miles away. 'I'm got nothing to say about anything,' he rasped. 'It's more than my life is worth to open my mouth. I've told you enough times, Jenny, that there's nothing we can do about our situation. If you put me back in that cell with Fenton, Deputy, and he thinks I've talked, he'll kill me for sure.'

'I'll keep you away from the rest of them,' Kendrick promised. 'You'll be protected.'

'And who's gonna protect you when Darra hears about this and comes into town with his bunch? Do you think you can stand up against them? Mister, they'd swallow you alive before break-fast, guts and all.'

Before Kendrick could answer, the street door was thrust open and a man entered the office hurriedly. Kendrick dropped a hand to his gun and

Armstrong did likewise.

'There's trouble in the saloon,' the man said quickly. There was a tremor in his tone and his face was showing extreme nervousness. 'Three trail hands are beating up the mayor. If you don't stop them pronto, they'll kill him. There's a dozen townsmen in the saloon, and no one has the nerve to step in and stop it.'

Kendrick recognized the man as a townsman, and went to the door. 'Put Jenny and her father in a separate cell, Jed,' he said to the jailer. 'And lock yourself in here until I get back.'

He departed quickly and the towns-man went with him.

'What happened in the saloon?' Kendrick asked as they hastened along the street.

'Those trail hands are troublemakers. It seems, from what I heard, that Mullin threw them out of his store this afternoon for trying to steal goods. They've been drinking steadily, and braced Mullin when he walked into the saloon. When he resisted, they started in on him.'

Kendrick reached the batwings of the saloon and paused to look in before entering. He saw at a glance that there were several trail hands engaged in the violence being offered to the town mayor. Mullin, almost unconscious, his face battered and bloody, was being held against the bar by two men while another was punching him. There were almost a dozen townsmen in the saloon, but no one was attempting to help Mullin, being cowed by a fourth trail hand, who was holding a drawn pistol.

Kendrick thrust open the batwings and entered. His boots thudded on the bare boards as he strode towards the little knot of men. The fourth trail hand was standing by, watching the beating with interest and, seeing Kendrick's approach, called a warning to his pards. The men released Mullin, who fell to the floor, and turned to face Kendrick.

The trail hand holding the gun made no attempt to use it, but one of the other three made the mistake of reaching for his pistol, and the movement set Kendrick into swift action. His six-shooter seemed to leap into his hand, and when the man continued his draw, Kendrick triggered a shot that blasted out the silence and rattled the bottles on the shelves behind the bar. His bullet took the man in the upper chest, its impact slamming him back against the bar where he paused, his gun only half-drawn. Then he slid to the floor beside the unconscious Mullin.

'Anyone else fancy his chance?' Kendrick demanded coolly, covering the trail hand who was still gripping his gun, although the muzzle of the weapon was now pointing at the floor. 'Use it or drop it, mister,' he advised.

The man opened his fingers and the .45 thumped in the sawdust. The other trail hands stood motionless, mesmerized by Kendrick's gun skill. Kendrick glanced at the tender, who was standing motionless behind the bar.

'You've got a shotgun under the bar, huh?' he demanded, and when the man nodded he said, 'Cover these men while I disarm them.'

The tender quickly lifted a 12-gauge Greener into view. Cocking the fearsome weapon, he pointed the twin muzzles at the trail hands. Kendrick stepped in close and quickly disarmed the men, tossing their weapons on the floor. He glanced at the tender, who seemed comfortable with the situation, and turned his attention to the unconscious town mayor.

Mullin was groaning. His face was swollen and bloody. Both eyebrows were leaking blood which streamed down his weathered face in gory lines. Kendrick shook his head. He looked around at the silent townsmen, who were standing in a line in the centre of the saloon.

'Someone fetch the doc, and make it quick,' he rapped. He straightened and turned his attention to the trail hand he had shot. The man was unconscious, and a splotch of blood marked the spot high on the right side of his chest where he had stopped the bullet. 'Let's get out of here,' he continued, addressing the trail hands. 'You're all under arrest. Pick up your pard and carry him to the jail. Don't give me any trouble. I'm looking for excuses to feed you some lead.'

The three unwounded trail hands picked up their pard and shuffled across the saloon towards the door. Kendrick followed closely, gun ready in his right hand, and he was close behind the group when they pushed through the batwings and stepped into the street. As he shouldered his way through the swing-door behind them, his reflexes hair-triggered, one of the men turned and attacked him, thrusting down Kendrick's gun and throwing a punch at his head.

But Kendrick was ready for trouble and averted the blow by raising his left shoulder to intercept it. The fist missed his jaw and he jerked his right knee into the man's groin. Then he swung his gunhand and crashed the barrel of his Colt across the man's face. Resistance faded instantly. The man fell to the street, while the other two trail hands stood transfixed, holding their wounded pard and gazing impassively at Kendrick.

'On your way,' Kendrick rapped. He bent and grasped the collar of the man he had struck and dragged him to his feet. The man was dazed by the blow he had received, and staggered as Kendrick propelled him along the street.

Several townsmen emerged from the saloon and followed the little group along the street. They had barely covered ten yards when several shots rang out, coming from the direction of the law office. Kendrick halted in shock. He peered through the shadows towards the sound of the shooting and caught a glimpse of movement as a number of saddle horses galloped out of town.

'Hold these men,' he rapped, and

started running along the street. He heard a confusion of voices at his back as the trail hands he had arrested turned on the unwilling townsmen, but he ignored it and ran to the jail, gun in hand, his mind already telling him that he had been tricked into leaving the place unattended.

His worst fears were confirmed when he reached the law office. The street door stood wide open, and he could see the figure of Jed Armstrong lying on the threshold. The sound of rapidly receding hoofs faded as he halted. He entered the office and dropped to one knee beside Armstrong, who was dead. Straightening, he approached the door leading into the cell block, which was open, and cold fear clutched at his heart. He did not know what to expect in the cells, and relief filled him when he entered and found the place deserted. He had expected to find Jenny Ensor and her father lying dead inside, but there was no sign of them. He stood looking at the empty cells, angry with himself for falling for the trick employed against him.

The townsmen who had been in the saloon came in at the door, two of them carrying the wounded trail hand. They put him down on the floor beside the body of Jed Armstrong.

'The other three got away,' one of the men said. 'There was no way we could stop them.'

'There'll be hell to pay for this,' another observed. 'Poor Jed Armstrong murdered! Just wait till Lorimer hears about it.'

Kendrick waved a hand wearily. 'Why don't you go back to the saloon?' he suggested. 'Leave that man on the floor, and send the doctor here if you see him.'

The men trooped out. Kendrick sat down at the desk, and Doc McKee came into the office, carrying his leather medical bag. He stopped in midstride at the sight of Armstrong stretched out on the floor, then dropped to one knee beside the man.

'Dead,' he said after a cursory examination. 'What's going on in this town, Chuck? I just looked at Mullin in the saloon. He's lucky to be alive. I've had him carried over to my place. What else have you got here?

Kendrick motioned to the trail hand lying on the floor and the doctor bent over the man.

'H'm, that'll take me about an hour to repair,' McKee said. 'I was looking forward to a quiet evening, but that's a thing of the past around here now.'

'It'll be all for tonight,' Kendrick said harshly. 'I reckon there's no one left in town who wants to have a go at the law.'

'I'll have a couple of men come for him.' McKee picked up his bag. 'They'll bring him over to my place.' He went to the door, then paused to look at Kendrick, who was sitting with his elbows propped on the desk and his chin cupped in his hands. 'If you reckon there'll be no more trouble around here tonight then the best thing you can do is hit the sack and get some rest. It's been a tough day for you.'

'You can say that again!' Kendrick got to his feet and began to pace the office, filled with a restlessness that overpowered him.

McKee watched him for a moment, then shook his head and departed. Kendrick stood at the door leading into the cell block, shaking his head at the thought of failing in his job. What was worse was the knowledge that he was responsible for Jed Armstrong's death. He turned and looked at the dead jailer, and the stark reality of the situation stabbed him deeply. He sighed and paced the office again, aware that there was nothing he could do until morning.

The door opened and two men looked into the office. 'Doc sent us,' one of them reported.

Kendrick pointed to the wounded trail hand. The men picked him up and carried him out. He had hardly closed the door behind the men when it was opened again and Pete Sanchez entered. The undertaker looked down at Jed Armstrong, shaking his head and tut-tutting.

'Get him out of here,' Kendrick said sharply.

'I got nowhere to put him.' Sanchez spoke apologetically. 'Since you came into town I've been run off my feet. Can I leave him in a cell? You got no prisoners now, I hear.'

Kendrick nodded. 'Sure. I'll give you a hand with him.'

They picked up the corpse, carried it into the cell block and placed it on a bunk.

'I'll pick him up first thing in the morning,' Sanchez promised.

'You'll know where to find him,' Kendrick said sourly.

The undertaker departed and Kendrick stood in the centre of the office, just looking around, feeling dispirited. He seemed to be no nearer to beating the lawlessness, and his thoughts flitted over the events that had occurred since his arrival in Red Mesa. The shock of having to kill Deke Hamley weighed heavily upon him. He set his teeth into his bottom lip while considering the situation. The bare bones of the plot to strip the range of cattle was obvious now, if what Jenny Ensor had said about it was true. Arch Kington, responsible for the rustling, was being backed by Blink Darra and his gang.

Unable to contain his restlessness, Kendrick left the office and went along the street to the saloon. He was in dire need of a drink, and accepted a whiskey on the house from the excited bartender. Sinking it at a gulp, he turned away from the bar and almost ran to the batwings, his thoughts suddenly animated. All the escaping prisoners would flee from the town, and keep running, if they had any sense. But Arch Kington was bossing the crooked operation, and would need to be around to oversee his set-up.

Kendrick went to the hotel, primed for trouble. Entering the lobby, he was struck by the air of desertion that seemed apparent. There was no one in evidence. The reception desk was not manned, and there was no reply when he rang the bell repeatedly. He went to the doorway of the small bar on the right of the lobby and found it dark and deserted. Not to be denied information, he pushed open the door of the private room at the rear of the lobby and entered to look for the reception clerk.

Shock struck him and he dropped a hand to his gun butt. A man was in the room, bound hand and foot to a chair, and there was a bandanna stuffed into his mouth.

8

Kendrick crossed to the man, removed the gag from his mouth and untied him. The clerk sprang to his feet, shocked and excited by his experience. He waved his arms and ranted about the way he had been treated.

'Calm down,' Kendrick advised him. 'Just tell me what happened.'

'Arch Kington, the cattle-buyer, came in with a couple of his tough trail hands. He wanted his money out of the safe, and when he saw what I keep in the safe he wanted that as well. I protested, but they dragged me in here and tied me. Kington is a thief, and I want him arrested.'

'He was under arrest until his trail hands busted him out of jail. But I'll catch up with him before long.' Kendrick was thinking swiftly, and wondered what had happened to Jenny

177

and her father. If Buster Fenton thought the girl had talked to the law then her future would be very short. 'I came here in the hope that Kington couldn't just pull out,' he mused. 'I reckoned he would have money to pick up. But I guess I'm too late to catch up with him. He'll have left town now, and I can't trail him until the sun shows.'

He left the hotel and walked along the street to the livery barn, concerned about Jenny Ensor. She had revealed something of the set-up that existed, and he wanted to help her if he could. It was a bad sign that the hardcases had taken her and Al Ensor along with them when they fled, but at least they had not been left dead in the cells.

He walked through the stable and looked out over the back lots, and his pulses raced when he saw that the Ensor wagon had gone. Straining his ears, he caught the sound of it jolting away into the darkness, heading west. He started running after it. But he soon realized that it was moving too fast for him to catch on foot, and the pain in his leg convinced him that he should return to the stable. Throwing his gear on the black, he was soon riding fast in pursuit, his spirits rising as he considered that all was not lost.

There was enough light from the stars to enable him to see to quite a distance, and he canted his head to catch the sounds of the wagon above the pounding of the black's hoofs. He soon spotted its dark shape moving west along the trail, and swung wide to approach it from one side. There was no sign of Fenton's horse around, and he remained hidden until he was certain there were no outriders. Then he drew his pistol and rode in close, coming up on the driver's right.

He recognized Jenny Ensor on the seat. She was whipping the horses. There was no sign of her father, and Kendrick assumed that Al was inside the wagon. Jenny suddenly spotted him and made a half-hearted reach for a pistol holstered on her right hip.

'Don't be stupid,' Kendrick called. 'Pull up and sit still.'

She obeyed immediately, dropping the reins when the team had halted to stand with heaving flanks.

'I didn't think I'd get away with it,' she muttered. 'But Dad and me didn't have anything to do with the jail break. Kington's trail hands came in after you'd been lured away. It was Fenton shot the jailer.'

'Where have the rest of them gone?' Kendrick demanded.

'You don't think they told me their plans, do you? Me and Pa are lucky to get away with our lives. Fenton thought we had spilled the beans and was ready to kill us. But Kington talked him out of it, after I promised to take the wagon on to Singing Springs. That's where I'm heading now.'

'Is your pa inside the wagon?'

'Nope. Fenton wanted to make sure I'd toe the line so he took Pa along with him. He doesn't trust us any more.'

'What are you supposed to do when

you reach Singing Springs?'

'Wait until I'm contacted. Pa will join me there, so they said.' She gazed anxiously at Kendrick. 'You're not going to stop me, are you?'

'Do you really want to get out of this crooked business?' he demanded. 'If you helped me come up with the Darra bunch I'd forget that you've been mixed up with the gang.'

'I swear me and Pa never did a wrong thing in our lives,' she protested. 'We always had one of the gang with us who did all the spying.'

'So prove your words by keeping me informed. Go to Singing Springs and do like they say. I'll be around, watching points, and you can let me know what the gang's plans are.'

'You'd trust me to do that?'

Kendrick grinned. 'I can always come up with you, Jenny, so don't try to play it smart. The law is getting wise to Darra now, and I reckon his days are numbered. If you don't wanta go down with him then you'll play it straight. I get the impression that you want your pa out of this mess.'

'My only concern is for Pa's safety,' she said firmly, 'and I won't do anything that might endanger him.'

'I wouldn't want anything bad happening to him,' Kendrick agreed. 'Play along with me. It's your pa's only chance, and even so, I'll have to try and swing it with the sheriff. He knows what your pa has been up to. It was him set me on your trail. So what do you say?'

'It looks like I got no choice,' she said despairingly. 'All right, I'll try to do what you say, but I don't figure there's much will come of it. Like I told you, we didn't have anything to do with the gang. The only time we saw an outlaw was when one of them came by to collect reports from Fenton. Now if you got hold of Fenton, and could make him talk, you might get somewhere. But he's one tough *hombre*. He'd rather die than talk. You'd have to beat him near to death, I guess, to unbutton his lip.'

'I'll bear that in mind.' Kendrick nodded. He was thinking that Jenny was at last coming down on his side. 'You got any idea where Fenton headed?'

'No.' She shook her head. 'Can I get on now? I got to get to Singing Springs fast. If I learn anything about the gang I'll leave a message for you at the law office in town.'

'Go on.' Kendrick waved a hand, and sat his horse while the girl snatched up the reins and quickly whipped the team into motion. The wagon jolted away, and he remained motionless until it had vanished into the indistinctness of the night. But he could hear the noise of its progress for a long time after it had departed.

Riding back to town, Kendrick was filled with misgiving. But he realized there was nothing he could do until morning. He stabled the black and walked back to the law office. He sat down resolutely at the desk, and tried to get comfortable in the chair. He

183

tipped his hat forward over his eyes and attempted to sleep. The night passed interminably, and he was standing impatiently in the doorway of the office, looking around gaunt-eyed, when the sun finally showed above the horizon to announce the proximity of a new day.

The little town came slowly to life, and Kendrick walked along the street to the restaurant, surprised, when he entered, to find that he was not the first customer of the day. The undertaker was eating breakfast, and did not pause; merely nodded his acknowledgement of Kendrick's entrance. Kendrick lifted a hand in reply and sat down at a table by the window. He ate breakfast quickly, hoping Sheriff Lorimer would show up soon, and was walking back along the street to the jail when he spotted a trio of riders coming into town, led by the diminutive sheriff.

He was standing in front of the law office when Lorimer reined in and gazed down at him. The sheriff looked tired. His face was gaunt, his eyes, as he squinted against the sun, almost lost in the pouches of flesh that surrounded them.

'Heck, Chuck, I sent you out on a little chore to get you out of my hair for a spell and keep you out of trouble, and you stirred up a real hornet's nest. Men have been killed nigh every mile between here and Clearwater Creek, the trading post was wrecked and Stafford killed, along with alleged outlaws, and then you ride in here and shoot my deputy. I hope to God you had a good reason for doing that. Hamley wasn't the best deputy in the world, but I figured he could handle Red Mesa. Heck, I was glad to get out of town when your report arrived for fear of what I'd learn next. So you reckon you've busted open the rustling business, huh? Well, let's hear it. What's happened around here since you wrote that report?'

Kendrick waited until the sheriff stepped down from his saddle. Lorimer dusted himself down and glanced at the two men who had accompanied him. One was Bill Watt, the chief deputy, who nodded bleakly when he caught Kendrick's eye.

'Take the horses down to the livery barn, Bill,' Lorimer instructed. 'Then get some breakfast, and bring me some grub when you come back here. I'll be in this darn office most of the day, I expect, trying to sort out the mess Chuck has landed us with. Frank, go along with Bill. He'll put you through your paces, and you'll get a deputy badge if you measure up.'

Kendrick watched the two men depart with the sheriff's horse. Lorimer pushed past him and entered the law office. Kendrick followed.

'Are you considering making Frank Harbin a deputy?' he demanded in some surprise.

'I reckon Frank will be a great help to us,' Lorimer said. He paused on the threshold of the office and looked around, smelling the pungency of charred wood and the last vestiges of burned powder from the shooting of the night before. 'This place could do with an airing,' he observed. 'Leave that door open, Chuck. You better get someone in to do some cleaning. It's like a pigsty in here.'

'I've been busy since I arrived,' Kendrick said harshly. 'Knee-deep in bad men, most of the time.'

'Yeah, well let's take a look at your prisoners.' Lorimer started for the door of the cell block, which was standing open. 'You should keep that door locked when the cells are occupied,' he reproved. 'How many times do I have to tell you?' Exasperation laced his voice.

'I ain't got any prisoners. They were busted out last night by a bunch of rustlers.' Defiance and defensiveness mingled in Kendrick's voice.

Lorimer halted in midstride, his mouth gaping as shock struck him. He gazed at Kendrick, gauged his attitude, and swallowed.

'All right,' he said, toning down the

rasp in his voice. 'Let's sit down and you can bring me up to date on what's happened since you wrote that report.'

He moved to the seat behind the desk, and as he sat down the undertaker stalked into the office, accompanied by two men.

'I've come for Jed Armstrong,' Sanchez said.

'Armstrong?' Lorimer looked around. 'Has he been on duty? We only call him in when there's an emergency.'

'If it wasn't an emergency last night then I'll never know what one looks like.' Kendrick's tone was like broken glass. 'Armstrong's dead in the cells.' He motioned for Sanchez to carry on, and the undertaker led his two helpers into the cell block. Drawing a deep breath, Kendrick launched himself into an account of events since he had written the report.

Lorimer listened in silence, his concentration unbroken by the under-taker and his men removing the body of Jed Armstrong. When Kendrick fell silent, the sheriff got to his feet and paced the office for several minutes. Finally, he halted behind Kendrick's chair and heaved a sigh.

'From what you've told me, I reckon there ain't a shred of evidence against anyone you had in the cells,' he mused. 'It's all hearsay, and we can't get a conviction on that alone.'

'I reckoned I had enough against everyone to hold them until you arrived this morning.' Kendrick suppressed a sigh. 'And there is proof against Kington robbing the hotel. The clerk is ready to lay charges. I told him to come and see you this morning. Those trail hands were on Kington's payroll, and I killed a number of them attacking this place. If that don't prove anything then I don't know nothing from nothing.'

'It's pointed us in the right direction, that's all,' Lorimer said grudgingly. 'So what about the Ensors? The girl was ready to spill the beans, you say? Then why did she run away?'

Kendrick explained the situation, and Lorimer shook his head. Kendrick was depressed by the sheriff's words, but swallowed his growing anger.

'I wouldn't trust father or daughter any further than I could throw them with both hands tied behind my back,' Lorimer said. 'But you're gonna trust them, huh? All right. Then you better head out for Singing Springs and do what you think is right. Just keep me informed of any developments. And if you catch up with the Darra gang then send to me for a posse before you try conclusions with them, huh?'

'You want me to ride out now?' Kendrick considered the thought, and was relieved by the knowledge that he could walk away from the situation enveloping him.

'Soon as you can saddle up. I guess I can straighten out this mess. But, before you go, what about Hamley? What made him pull his gun on you?'

Kendrick shook his head. 'I figure he was in with the outlaws and rustlers. Fenton gave him orders about something, and when I mentioned it to

Hamley he drew on me.'

'I'll get to the bottom of it,' Lorimer promised. 'Hit the trail now, and for God's sake don't do in Singing Springs what you did here yesterday.'

'So if I walk into something that ain't right you want me to close my eyes to it, huh?' Kendrick shook his head. 'If you don't trust me to do my job properly then you only got to hold out your hand and I'll drop my badge into it. I'm fed up to my back teeth as it is. I'm ready to quit.'

'Now there ain't no cause for you to take that attitude, Chuck.' Lorimer's tone changed instantly. 'You have done good so far, and when you've got more experience in law-dealing you'll be top man in the department. Go to it, son, and good luck.'

Kendrick left the office, undecided about continuing. But he wanted to face Blink Darra's gang, and Trig Weevil in particular, and the best way he could achieve that was by wearing a law badge. He went to the store to replenish his supplies and came face to face with Mrs Mullin, a tall, thin woman with piercing blue eyes.

'How's the mayor this morning?' he asked.

'He's come through it pretty good,' she replied. 'Thank Heaven you were in town last night. If Hamley had been in charge there's no telling what would have happened. Tom owes his life to you, and he wants to see you. I was about to come over to the jail to fetch you.'

'Is he fit enough to see visitors? From what I saw of him last night, I thought he'd be unable to see or speak for a couple of weeks at least.'

'He's a tough man, is Tom. I'd better take you in to see him or I'll never hear the last of it, especially if you're leaving town now.'

Kendrick followed the woman into the back of the store and through to the living-quarters. She conducted him into a bedroom, where the town mayor was lying propped up in bed. Mullin's head was bandaged, his face swollen and bruised extensively, his eyes mere slits in the tortured flesh surrounding them.

'Howdy, Chuck,' he said stiffly, having trouble articulating his words, his voice slurring as he tried to get his tongue around them. 'Glad you could come. I need to talk to you. I owe you a vote of thanks for saving me last night. What happened was a real eye-opener to the problems we got in Red Mesa. I guess I should have spoken up before, but with a man like Hamley holding the reins of the local law there wasn't much I could do. But there are a couple of men in town who, I know for a fact, are working with the bad men, and I'll give evidence against them should you need a witness. I been holding back too long. I've got to speak out if this town is to be rid of bad men.'

'We could do with some public-spirited men to stand up and be counted,' Kendrick said. 'But the sheriff is in town now, and he's taken over the local law. I'm on my way out to handle

193

another job.' His tone hardened. 'I got a date with some bad men of my own, and I've been waiting a long time to face them.'

'The Darra gang.' Mullin nodded, and groaned at the movement. 'I know your story, Chuck, and you have my best wishes. Do you know where the gang is hiding?'

Kendrick shook his head. 'I'd give my eye-teeth for that information,' he said.

'Pick up Hank Tropman, the bank guard, and try to squeeze some truth out of him. I overheard him talking to a hardcase a couple of weeks ago, offering to sell information to the gang. I'm ready to testify in court, if necessary.'

'You actually heard him say that?'

'It's the gospel truth. I couldn't tell Hamley because I suspected him of working in with the rustlers, and I just didn't get around to sending word to the sheriff. I guess I hoped the situation would go away if I ignored it. But I know better now. Nothing will change around here unless I stand up and make it happen. And while you're at it, pick up Mal Keane. He works as a swamper in Ryan's saloon and mixes with the rough element in town. I've heard whispers that he's got a hand in the rustling. He sure was friendly with Arch Kington when that crooked cattle-buyer rode in.'

'I'll pass on your information to the sheriff,' Kendrick said. 'He's handling the law hereabouts now.'

'I'd rather you didn't tell him about it.' Mullin shook his head, stifling a groan as he did so. 'I've heard some pretty bad talk about Lorimer, and there's no smoke without fire, so they say. I wouldn't trust him these days. I hate to say this, but Abe's living on borrowed time. He should have quit a long time ago, but clung on to his job, and I think he's been lining his nest these last few years.'

Kendrick gazed at Mullin with disbelief in his eyes.

'I hope you've got proof to back up your words,' he said. 'There ain't been a straighter man than Abe Lorimer.'

'That was before he got old and bitter.' Mullin sighed and pressed a hand to his forehead. 'I guess I'm running off too much at the mouth,' he said tiredly. 'But I'm trying to repay you for what you did for me last night. What you do about it is your business, I guess.'

'Thanks.' Kendrick turned to the door. 'You better rest up now. I'll talk to you again when I get back from my trip.'

'Good luck,' Mullin said, and subsided with a groan.

Kendrick went back into the store. He collected a sack of supplies and went on to the livery barn. The town seemed quiet — too quiet, he thought. He saddled up, tied his supplies behind the cantle and filled his canteen at the pump. Then he rode along the street, his mind seething with Mullin's information, and wondering what he should do about it.

Passing the bank, he saw Hank

Tropman, the bank guard, standing just inside the entrance. The man stared at him, unsmiling, his features set in deep lines. Kendrick reined in and stepped down from his saddle, pausing for a moment while a twinge of pain racked his leg. He went into the bank, and saw Tropman drop his hand to the butt of his holstered gun as a questioning light dawned in the man's eyes.

'Everything quiet around here, Tropman?' he asked.

'Sure.' Tropman was surly. 'Why shouldn't it be? What's on your mind, coming in here this early in the morning?'

'All the trouble that's hit the town in the last twenty-four hours. Have you seen anyone suspicious hanging around the bank? There's talk that the outlaws are showing an interest in Red Mesa.'

'Half the men in town look suspicious to me, and anyone of them could be an outlaw, for all I know.' Tropman grinned. Then his heavy face sobered. 'I ain't seen no strangers around, if that's

197

what you mean. I heard that your trouble last night was caused by them hardcases who run the rustling business.'

'Where did you hear that?' Kendrick countered.

'Everyone in town is talking about it this morning.' Tropman scowled again. 'You can't talk to Monroe, if that's what you're here for. He's gone to see the doc. Not feeling too well.'

'There are some badmen around town, acting like respectable folk, who think they're safe from the law,' Kendrick remarked. 'But they won't be feeling too well when we come up with them. See you around, Tropman.'

Kendrick departed, not knowing what to make of Tropman. He glanced over his shoulder and saw the bank guard watching him intently, then swung into the saddle, cursing the pain that stabbed through his leg. He rode on. Reaching the jail, he saw Abe Lorimer sitting outside as if he were back in Clearwater Creek, and he wondered about the lawman, unable to believe that the sheriff had turned to crime in the last stage of his illustrious career.

He shook his head at the thought, finding it too hard to swallow. Lorimer raised a hand to him as he passed, and Kendrick turned aside on impulse and rode up to where the lawman was seated. Lorimer arose, pulled his chair around into a rapidly dimishing patch of shade, and sat down again as Kendrick reined up in front of him. Kendrick eyed him as if he had never seen the sheriff before, such was his suspicion.

'I thought you'd be long gone by now,' Lorimer said.

'I had a chinwag with Tom Mullin. He's in a bad way from the beating he got last night. I reckon you should drop by and talk to him, Abe. Ask him about Hank Tropman and Mal Keane. He reckons both men should be in jail.'

'Is that a fact?' Lorimer narrowed his eyes as he gauged Kendrick's mood.

Then he nodded. 'All right. I'll go see him. But Mullin is a great one for sticking his nose into men's business since he became mayor. He's worse than an old widder-woman who's got nothing better to do than exercise her tongue. I ain't surprised he got a beating last night. Must have come down heavily on someone's toes with that mouth of his.'

Kendrick reined his horse away, disliking the tone in Lorimer's voice, and continued along the street, his relief growing by leaps and bounds as he left the town. He hit the trail for Singing Springs, letting the horse find its own pace, and was relieved when he spotted the tracks of the Ensor wagon moving in the same direction. The way things had been going, he wouldn't be surprised if Jenny double-crossed him in some way and took advantage of his good nature by setting him up for the outlaws or the rustlers.

He drowsed as he rode, for he had not slept well during the night, and the heat of the sun on his back seemed to draw the vitality from his body. But the pounding hoofs of several riders alerted him. He straightened quickly in the saddle and looked around to see four riders coming towards him from the direction of Singing Springs. He dropped his hand to the butt of his pistol and gazed at them suspiciously until he recognized Ben Slater, the Bar S rancher, and Jake Sarn, the ranch foreman. The quartet came up fast, raising dust, and reined in before him.

'You looked like you was taking it easy,' Slater rasped, cuffing back his Stetson and wiping his sweating fore-head. 'But then you can afford to when folk like us ride out to do your job for you. We came up with a big bunch of rustlers just before sundown last night. They were hazing a herd of mebbe seven hundred head of Bar S and Circle B stock. We went into them bald-headed as they approached Dead Horse Canyon and shot the hell outa them. Five went down, and we lost four men, two dead. So what have you been doing since I last saw you?'

Kendrick explained tersely and saw incredulity dawn in the faces of the cattlemen. He gave them the unvarnished truth of what had occurred since leaving them at the burning Bar S ranch and, when he lapsed into silence, Ben Slater was at a loss for words, his gaze filled with ungrudging admiration.

'So it looks like Arch Kington is running the rustling,' Kendrick concluded, 'and, from what I heard, he's in cahoots with the Darra gang.'

'Hell, I saw Kington on the trail this morning, heading into Singing Springs,' Slater said. 'Him and a bunch of his trail hands. We'd dropped off our men in town who were shot in the fracas, and two of the wounded rustlers. We'll ride back with you and give Kington his come-uppance.'

'Nope.' Kendrick shook his head. 'You better ride on into Red Mesa and report to Lorimer. He'll wanta know about your doings. Come on to Singing

Springs afterwards, if you like. But it won't help matters if you go off half-cocked. We need to get the whole bunch when we strike.' He paused, then asked: 'Have you seen anyone else on the trail to Singing Springs?'

'Only the pedlar's gal, driving that wagon, and she sure was in a helluva hurry, laying into her team with a whip. She passed us like a bat out of hell, and you could hear those pots and pans rattling and clanging a mile away. Scared the hell outa our broncs. I reckon she'll need fresh horses when she gets to where she's going.'

Slater touched the brim of his hat with a gnarled forefinger and rode on, taking his hard-bitten men with him. Kendrick gazed after them for some moments before riding on at a faster pace. He was impatient now to reach Singing Springs, his eyes glinting as he considered his chances of catching up with Arch Kington and the rest of his prisoners who had escaped from Red Mesa.

A bullet crackled past his left ear, coming from behind. He kicked his feet clear of the stirrups and dived sideways out of the saddle, trying to spare his left leg. But he hit the ground with considerable force, and clenched his teeth at the pain that coursed through his limb. The sound of the shot came faintly to his ears, and a series of echoes fled to the distant horizon. A second shot struck the ground a bare inch from his right elbow, and he grunted at the effort as he rolled into a depression and prepared to fight.

With his pistol cocked and ready in his hand, he raised himself up for a look around, and another slug struck the ground just in front of him, so close that dust flew into his eyes. He cursed and ducked, then looked around for the black, but the animal had moved out of danger and stood yards away, quietly cropping the lush grass. Kendrick relaxed and lay still, hoping to draw the ambusher out of cover, He listened intently to the fading echoes, and when silence returned he felt his nerves tighten to an intolerable degree.

Sweat dripped down his face. He was aware of the heavy pounding of his heart as he waited, and gripped his pistol, hoping for at least a half-chance of survival should his attacker come close to inspect his apparent kill.

9

Kendrick's left leg became cramped as he waited. The silence now was intense, dragging at his nerves. He tried to roll on to his right side to ease his leg, and must have exposed himself because the rifle fired again, sounding much closer. A bullet smacked into the ground by his left elbow. He tried to judge the direction from which the slug had come, and tensed to make a dash to better cover, but the niggling pain in his leg anchored him and he feared he could not move fast enough to avoid a bullet.

Sensing that he could wait no longer, he cocked the pistol and prepared to move. He knew the direction the ambusher was coming from, and reared up, gun lifting. He saw a man approaching, and recognized Hank Tropman, who lifted a rifle to his shoulder. Kendrick triggered his pistol. The short weapon blasted a split second before Tropman's rifle cracked, and the bank guard was actually falling when his 44.40 rifle slug tore through the thick flesh of Kendrick's left arm above the elbow. Staggering backwards, Kendrick kept his gun lined up on Tropman but held his fire. Tropman was crumpling to the ground, blood on his shirt front, his rifle falling aside.

Kendrick paused to check his arm. The bullet had gouged the flesh just below the bicep. Blood was dripping, but he realized that the wound was not serious. He thrust his gun into its holster and removed his neckerchief, shaking dust from it before binding his arm. His gaze did not leave Tropman, who was lying on his back with both arms outflung.

He went forward, drawing his gun once more, and covered the inert figure until he was standing over it. A splotch of blood was spreading over Tropman's shirt, almost dead centre, and the man's eyes flickered as Kendrick bent over him.

'Why did you come for me, Tropman?' Kendrick asked.

Blood dribbled from a corner of Tropman's mouth. His eyes revealed deep shock. His breathing was fast and heavy, as if he had been running.

'When you came to me in town I could tell you were on to me,' he gasped. 'I saw it in your eyes. Who told you?' His right hand came up and grasped Kendrick's wrist. He attempted to pull himself into a sitting position but the effort was too much for him and he slumped back. 'Who told you?' he repeated.

'Tom Mullin.'

Tropman grinned and blood streamed from his mouth. 'That busybody! I might have known. I had to come for you. But I should have known it was hopeless. You've done for me.' He closed his eyes and relaxed, and Kendrick thought he had died, but his eyes opened again, and now there was a distant light in them, as if he was looking beyond death and could see what was there waiting for him.

'You were in with the outlaws,' Kendrick prompted. 'Get it off your chest before you go, Tropman. Tell me where Darra is hiding out.'

'You won't have to look for him.' Tropman's voice wavered and grew fainter. 'He'll come for you when he's ready. I sent word to him last night about you. He'll be waiting somewhere along your trail.'

Tropman's voice faded into silence and his fingers on Kendrick's wrist lost their desperate strength. He relaxed with a long sigh as his last breath was exhaled. His legs tremored convulsively, and then he was still.

Kendrick arose, his face grim. He glanced around, carefully checking all approaches. Holstering his gun, he limped to where his horse was grazing and mounted to ride back the way Tropman had come, looking for the man's horse. He found the animal in a draw, took it back to load Tropman's body across the saddle, then continued to Singing Springs.

It was evening when he sighted the town, shimmering in the heat. The sun was reaching down to the horizon. Kendrick was hungry and thirsty. He dismounted and made camp in a thicket, knee-hobbling his horse to prevent it straying, and tied Tropman's mount to a twig. He ate cold food and drank brackish water from his canteen. He did not want to arrive in Singing Springs until after sundown, and rested until shadows began to crawl into his surroundings. But although his body was resting his brain was alive with conjecture.

Hank Tropman had said he'd sent word to the outlaws the previous evening. That meant someone must have ridden from Red Mesa to Singing Springs, and Kendrick had to control his impatience, aware that he might be on the edge of a breakthrough. He waited until night began to fall, then rode into the little town, leading the horse carrying Tropman's body.

The main street was densely shadowed when he entered it, and he turned into the livery barn on the right. He put his horse into a stall and attended to its needs, then dragged Tropman off his mount and took care of the animal in like manner. He dumped Tropman's body behind a pile of hay, checked his pistol, and went into the town.

Lights shone from many buildings along the long main street, creating a strip of shadow along its centre. Kendrick knew the place well, had often ridden in when his duties brought him into this part of the county. He moved furtively along the line of buildings on the right, and paused at Jenson's saloon to peer inside, hoping to spot some of the men who had escaped from the jail in Red Mesa. A piano was being played loudly inside the big room, which contained some five men lining the long bar, with a further dozen seated around three of the tables, gambling.

Kendrick ran his eye over the faces at the bar, and was disappointed not to see any of those men he was looking for. He checked the men at the gaming-tables — those whose faces he could see — and shook his head. None had been in Red Mesa the evening before. Turning away, he had to sidestep a dark figure that was approaching the saloon. The man caught Kendrick with an elbow in passing, and muttered an apology as he thrust open the batwings. Kendrick faded into the shadows and went on along the street, making for the law office, which was situated beside the bank. He was on edge, hoping against hope that he would have some of the breaks after the way the situation had turned out at Red Mesa. One good thing about Singing Springs, he thought, was that he could trust the deputy, Pete Bardon.

He entered the law office and found Bardon sitting behind the desk. The deputy looked up, and grinned a welcome, getting to his feet and coming around the desk with an outstretched hand. Tall and slender of build, his blue eyes shone with pleasure as they shook hands.

'I got word you were coming today, Chuck,' he said. 'This is a real pleasure.'

'Who told you?' Kendrick's eyes narrowed. 'Who came in from Red Mesa?'

'Jenny Ensor showed up early this afternoon.'

'Anyone else ride in from Red Mesa?' Kendrick was thinking of Hank Tropman sending word to the outlaws.

'Can't say I've seen anyone. You expecting someone to turn up?'

'I'll take a look around later. While I think of it, Pete, I dumped the body of Hank Tropman behind a pile of hay in the livery barn.' He explained what had happened on the trail, and saw shock on Bardon's face. He nodded. 'Yeah, bad things have been happening in Red Mesa. How have you been doing here? Any trouble?'

'Not a thing. Anything I can do to help?'

Kendrick mentioned men he was looking for and Bardon shook his head.

'I ain't seen any of those folks,' he said. 'Jenny is the only one I spotted. She came rolling into town in that wagon Ensor drives around in, but I ain't seen hide nor hair of him. Come to think of it, Jenny seemed like she was worrying about something.'

'Any idea where she is now?'

'She left the wagon back of the livery barn. Then she met up with the guy who's been travelling around with Al Ensor. Buster Fenton. He's been travelling with them a couple of years now. I did hear tell that Jenny was planning to marry Buster, but I don't figure that would work out. She's too fiery for any man, and Buster don't look the type to settle down.'

Kendrick rubbed the spot on his head where Jenny had raised a lump, which was still painful. 'I know what you mean,' he said. 'That gal sure is a handful. Did you see Fenton ride in? I was wondering if he came alone.'

'Didn't see him arrive. Can't say I like the look of him. Seems a slippery cuss to me. I hope you're not bringing trouble to town, Chuck. It's been nice and peaceful since your last visit. Did you catch up with that horse-thief you chased through here six months ago?'

'Yeah. I got him. He was strung up in Clearwater Creek after his trial.' Kendrick shrugged. 'As to trouble, well, there's a lot of it around right now and I seem to be knee-deep in it. I'll try not to disturb your town, Pete, but there's work to be done, and I'd better make a start. Take care of Tropman's body, will you?'

'Sure thing, and don't hesitate to call me if you need any help.'

Kendrick smiled and departed. He went back to the stable and passed through it to check the back lot. When he saw the Ensor wagon he dropped a hand to the butt of his pistol and walked to it. The shadows were dense.

He moved slowly, alert for trouble. So Buster Fenton was in town. He wondered how many more of those who had got out of jail were around.

There was no one at the wagon, and Kendrick stood in the darkness thinking about the situation. The evening breeze sighed quietly around him, its breath warm. The silence was punctuated by small natural sounds. He heard the Ensor team cropping grass nearby, and leaned a shoulder against the side of the wagon. A few moments later, as he was considering moving on, he heard the sound of a woman's voice suddenly raised in sharp protest, and stiffened into alertness. Two figures materialized out of the gloom as he recognized Jenny Ensor's voice.

'I told you to stay clear of me, Buster, until you can tell me where my father is,' Jenny was saying. 'I'm not gonna do a blamed thing for you or anyone else until Pa is loose, so don't try to sweet-talk me. You promised me Pa would be here, free as a bird, if I brought the wagon from Red Mesa. Well, I've kept my side of the bargain, and all you can do is make more promises. How do I know Pa is still alive? Do you think I trust you and that bunch you ride with? None of them cares what happens to anyone.'

'Calm down, Jenny,' Fenton replied as they approached the wagon. 'I can't work miracles. Thornton is holding on to Al until we get things sorted out. There's no telling what will happen with Chuck Kendrick on the loose. I'll bet he's heading here this very minute, and we sure don't need trouble from him at this time.'

'Just tell me where my pa is,' Jenny responded. 'Let me see him. I want to see for myself that he's still in one piece. Thornton's trail hands are mighty violent men.'

'They figured Al was ready to talk to the law about them,' Fenton rasped. 'I wouldn't be able to save you or Al if you did spill the beans. There's a lot at stake right now. Just play it cool and you'll get your way, but kick over the traces and that'll be the end of it.'

'Where is Pa being held? You can tell me that, can't you?'

'You wouldn't know the place if I did tell you. He's not at the hideout. And I can't take you out to where he is now. I got things to do around town.'

'Then get on and do them and stop bothering me. I need to sleep. I was driving that wagon all last night. And what was so important that I had to come here non-stop? Nothing is happening here. You just told me to go to bed and forget about everything.'

'We needed you out of Clearwater Creek before Kendrick could drop on to you. Now you're here, so stop bitching and do like you're told. My job is hard enough without you adding to it. You can see Al tomorrow, if you behave yourself. Don't upset the apple-cart now or you'll never see him again. The gang is playing for high stakes. You know what they're like. Cross them and you'll pay for it. No one is safe when they set their minds to do something. Heck, Blink Darra would shoot his own mother if he thought he could benefit by her death. Wise up to the situation, Jenny. You're being watched, and if you put a foot wrong now, well, I don't need to tell you what will happen, do I?'

Jenny did not reply. She went to the back of the wagon and reached inside for a lamp. Kendrick eased back into the shadows as she struck a match. Fenton grasped the girl's shoulder. She tried to shake him off but he held her.

'Pay heed to my warning,' Fenton said harshly. 'I got to go now. I'll come and see you in the morning. Go to bed and stay in the wagon until the sun shows.'

He turned and faded into the darkness, his boots rapping the hard ground. Kendrick moved back into denser shadows and turned away. He needed to follow Fenton, and set off behind the man. Fenton reached the street and walked swiftly towards the saloon, and Kendrick was like a shadow as he followed.

Fenton pushed through the batwings and entered the noisy bar-room. Kendrick went to a window and peered in. He watched Fenton go to the bar and call for a drink. Two hardcases arose from a nearby table and made a beeline for Fenton. Kendrick narrowed his eyes as he studied the men, fancying that one of them had been in Red Mesa the previous evening. He would have given a month's pay to be able to eavesdrop on the trio's conversation, but he wanted to remain unseen and contented himself with watching.

The two hardcases left Fenton abruptly and came out of the saloon. Kendrick watched them walk along the street towards the stable, and his concern for Jenny grew. Glancing at Fenton at the bar, he decided the man looked as if he planned to stay in the saloon for a spell. He set off after the two hardcases. He was just behind them when they passed through the stable, and drew his pistol when they moved towards the now darkened wagon. He did not want to advertise his presence in town but could not stand by if Jenny was attacked.

The two men stopped by the wagon, one of them calling out to Jenny, using her name. Kendrick closed in, hugging the side of the wagon. He heard Jenny reply peevishly; she evidently thought Fenton had returned.

'What do you want now?' she demanded. 'How am I supposed to get some sleep if you keep coming back to bother me?'

'We got news of your pa,' one of the men said. 'Come on out here and make it quick. Your old man is in danger.'

Kendrick heard the tarpaulin cover being pulled aside, and then Jenny's voice sounded loud and clear.

'Do you know where my pa is?' she demanded. Then she paused, evidently looking over the pair. 'Say, neither of you is Buster Fenton. What's going on? Who are you men?'

'You're coming with us,' one of them said, and grasped Jenny's arm, almost hauling her out of the wagon.

Jenny screeched like a wet hen, and Kendrick heard a hollow metallic clang as she picked up a saucepan and lashed out with it. She struck again, and one of the men dropped to his knees. The other uttered an oath and sprang into the wagon to grapple with her.

Kendrick stepped around the end of the wagon and struck with the long barrel of his pistol, laying it along the head of the man already on the ground. Then he reached up with his left hand and secured a grip on the belt of the man who had climbed into the wagon. He dragged the man out of the vehicle and hit him across the left temple with the pistol, then ducked as Jenny came at him with an upraised saucepan.

'Take it easy, Jenny,' Kendrick called. 'It's me, Kendrick. I've been watching out for you. Fenton sent these two men. Have you got any idea what they want?'

'They said something about my

father being in trouble,' Jenny said.

'I heard what they said. Do you know them?'

'I've seen them around. They're some of the hardcases Fenton mixes with. I wonder why he sent them after me?'

'They didn't come to enquire after your health.' Kendrick spoke grimly. 'I think we'd better go and ask Fenton himself.'

'What about these two?' Jenny looked down at the two men.

Kendrick bent over the men, removed their belts, and tied their wrists together with rope that Jenny produced.

'We'll leave them here,' he said as he straightened. 'I'll get the local deputy to run them in. Are you ready to face Fenton?'

'If Buster sent those men to harm me then I've got no choice,' Jenny replied. 'But how do I know what was in their minds?'

'I think you do know, one way or the other,' he replied. 'If you're not concerned for yourself then think of your pa. They're holding him hostage now. What will happen to him when they decide that he's no further use to them?'

'Let's go see Fenton,' Jenny said firmly, and Kendrick nodded, certain that she was making the right choice.

They went back through the stable to the street and walked to the saloon. Two riders were dismounting at the hitching rail outside as they arrived, and when they passed through the batwings, Jenny, catching a glimpse of their faces in the lamplight, clutched at Kendrick's arm and uttered an exclamation.

'Those two are in Darra's gang,' she said sharply. 'I've seen them before.'

'Then we'd better not go in there until they leave.' Kendrick grasped Jenny's arm and drew her into deep shadow. 'And I'll need to follow them when they leave. I've never been this close to the Darra gang before and I'm not missing this chance. That gang has come to the end of its trail.'

'Follow them and you'll be making a big mistake.' Jenny's eyes reflected lamplight as she glanced at him. 'I might be able to get you into the gang's hideout, but you'd never make it on your own.'

'I thought you said you didn't know where the hideout is.'

'Those two men coming after me at the wagon improved my memory a lot,' she replied brazenly. 'But I wouldn't take you into the hideout by yourself. You'd need a posse backing you to stand any kind of a chance against Darra and his gang.'

'Just show me into the hideout and leave the rest to me,' he retorted.

'I think my pa has been taken to the hideout,' Jenny said. 'It's about ten miles from here — a horse ranch where the outlaws rest up when they're in this area. The place is run as a legitimate business, managed for the gang, and they've got more than one spread around the country. This one is on the edge of the desert so it's easy for the gang to get into it and out again.'

'There's plenty of time to get me there before sunup,' Kendrick mused.

'Not so fast. Rein in your horse, Deputy. If I took you out there now, you'd be dead come morning, and that wouldn't help you or me. Let's get Fenton on his own and sweat some talk out of him.'

'Wait here until I get back.' Kendrick was prickling with eagerness. 'I'll get the local law in on this and we'll take everyone connected with the gang. Once they're behind bars we can work on them.'

'Don't waste time,' Jenny told him. 'I got the feeling that you've got to strike now or your chance will be gone.'

Kendrick looked through the window into the saloon and saw the two newcomers talking with Fenton, who was leaning against the bar as if he intended remaining there all night. He turned away to go to the law office but paused and grasped Jenny's arm.

'I think you'll be safer in jail until

we've handled Fenton and his pards,' he decided. 'Come along.'

Jenny turned into a wildcat at his words, launching herself at him with clawing fingers, and Kendrick, despite his bulk and strength, found her almost impossible to hold. After a tussle he solved the problem by encircling her arms with his own and throwing her across his left shoulder. She railed at him, kicking and struggling, as he carried her along the street.

When they entered the law office, Jenny subsided immediately. Pete Bardon, the town deputy, was bending over a man who was lying on his back in front of the desk, and Jenny uttered a wailing cry as Kendrick set her upon her feet.

'Pa!' she screeched, and ran forward to the apparently unconscious man.

Kendrick frowned as he went forward to look down at Al Ensor. The man had been roughed up. His face was bruised and blood had dribbled from his nose. But the bloodstain on the front of his shirt, which had been holed by a bullet, looked more serious.

'He came staggering in here a few minutes ago,' Bardon said, 'and collapsed as I was trying to get some details from him. But all he could say was that he wanted to see you, Kendrick. I sent a man to summon the doctor and to fetch you. But I reckon Ensor is breathing his last.'

The door of the office was thrust open and Kendrick spun to face it, his pistol leaping into his hand. Two men crowded in through the doorway, and Kendrick lowered his gun when he recognized the two ranchers, Ben Slater of the Bar S and Frank Belmont of the Circle B. Both men grinned when they saw him, and Kendrick shook his head in surprise when he noted that each was wearing a deputy badge on his shirt front.

'Lorimer sent us to back you up,' Slater said. 'He's certain you're near to bringing the Darra gang to justice and reckons our crews together can give you enough fire-power to do it. We've played it smart. We've got fifteen men between us, and we've left them in cover by the Ensor wagon back of the livery barn. And we found a couple of men hogtied in that wagon. They was making a helluva racket to attract attention.'

'What did you do with them?' Kendrick demanded.

'Nothing,' Belmont said. 'They're still in the wagon, with a couple of the boys watching them.'

'Can you use us?' Slater demanded. 'Lorimer told us the outlaws and the rustlers are working together. We haven't had much luck hunting the rustlers by ourselves, and we'd sure like to be in on the round-up you're making.'

'Sure thing.' Kendrick heaved a sigh as his mind flitted over the situation. 'Have those two men at the wagon brought in here quietly. Then split your men into two groups. Cover the front of the saloon along the street, one party at the front and the other at the back. Stay under cover, but arrest anyone trying to leave. I'm going in there shortly to make some arrests, and I don't want anyone getting away to carry word to the outlaws.'

Both ranchers grinned and turned away eagerly, hurrying to obey his orders, and Kendrick steeled himself with the knowledge that at last he was in a position to confront the Darra gang and settle the long-standing score they owed his father.

'Pete, you'd better stay here and handle this,' he said. 'Don't let Jenny leave under any circumstances. I'll need her shortly.'

Bardon nodded and Kendrick departed, walking along the street to position himself in the shadows in front of the saloon. He waited stolidly for the cowhands to arrive, impatience and eagerness gripping him. Silence enveloped him, but he could already smell gunsmoke, and itched to get into action. But he contained his feelings, standing in an alley-mouth, watching the batwings of the saloon, allowing the minutes to pass interminably. He was certain now that nothing could go wrong, and braced himself for what was to come.

When he heard the boots of several men coming towards him he checked that they were the cowhands, and grinned when he saw Ben Slater leading half a dozen intent figures. He moved out of cover and looked through a saloon window, nodding when he saw Fenton still standing at the bar inside, accompanied by the two hardcases Jenny had identified as gang members.

'What do you want us to do?' Slater demanded when he reached Kendrick's side.

'Back my play,' Kendrick replied, drawing his pistol and checking its mechanism. 'I'm gonna arrest some hardcases in here.'

'Sure thing.' Slater was grinning.

Kendrick went to the batwings and shouldered them open. He strode into the saloon with his deadly gun levelled in his hand and the tough cowhands crowding closely behind. It was clean-up time.

10

The noise in the saloon ceased abruptly when the armed men entered. Kendrick, watching Fenton and the two hardcases, saw all three reach for their guns, and shouted a warning for them to throw up their hands. Fenton snarled defiantly and continued his draw. Kendrick's teeth clicked together when he saw the intention. His Colt blasted and, as a plume of smoke billowed from the weapon, Fenton staggered under the hammerblow of a .45 slug smashing into his chest. He fell sideways against the two hardcases, who had frozen into immobility at Kendrick's grim warning, and they remained motionless while Fenton slumped to the floor and lay still.

As the echoes of the shot faded slowly, Frank Belmont and the rest of the cowboys crowded in through the rear door, all holding guns, and formed a watchful line across the saloon. Kendrick lowered his pistol and stood motionless, eyes glinting as he considered Fenton's decision to die. He motioned to Belmont, and the Circle B rancher came forward.

'This is the law,' Kendrick said loudly as he glanced around the big room. 'Just stand still while we run a check on you. Frank, disarm those two at the bar and take them along to the law office. Put them in the cells.'

Belmont beckoned two of his men and they went forward. The two outlaws were marched out of the saloon, and Kendrick turned his attention to the bartender.

'Point out any strangers in here,' he said.

The tender roused himself and looked around. His eyes were glassy with shock. He pointed silently to three of the men present, who were arrested and hurried away to the jail by some of the possemen. Satisfied, Kendrick started for the door, holstering his gun as he did so, and one of the possemen, who had been positioned on the sidewalk, thrust through the batwings.

'There's a bunch of riders coming into town,' he reported.

Kendrick went out to the sidewalk and peered into the uncertain darkness along the street. Six riders were coming in, and he dropped a hand to his gunbutt as he awaited their arrival. Ben Slater and the possemen emerged from the saloon and spread out along the sidewalk, guns ready in their hands.

'Hold everything,' Kendrick warned. 'That's Abe Lorimer coming in.'

The silence was intense as the sheriff rode up and slid stiffly out of his saddle. He came to confront Kendrick's big figure, nodding as he looked around.

'Looks like you've got everything under control,' he said. 'We heard shooting as we came in. Anyone I know?'

'Buster Fenton decided to quit.'

Kendrick spoke tersely. 'We were rounding up the undesirables before getting down to the real business.'

'Which is?' Lorimer prompted.

'The Darra gang.' Kendrick experienced a rush of emotion as he spoke.

'You sure cleaned up Red Mesa.' Lorimer grinned. 'And you've got enough men here to take care of every badman this side of the Mexican border. Any word on the Darra outfit?'

'Not yet, but I'll be moving out soon as I get a line on Darra.'

'Let me know if you discover Darra's hideout.' Lorimer turned to the saloon. 'We'll get ourselves a drink before looking around. It's a thirsty ride from Red Mesa. See you in the law office shortly, Chuck. You're doing all right, son, but keep pushing.'

Kendrick frowned as he started along the street to the law office. He was thinking of the suspicion Tom Mullin had planted in his mind back in Red Mesa. Was the sheriff in with the outlaws? He shook his head, believing that the truth would come out when the final showdown occurred. He paused when Ben Slater called to him.

'What do you want us to do now, Chuck?' the Bar S rancher demanded.

'Be ready to ride out at a moment's notice. Get supplies for several days. Make sure your horses are ready to travel. Keep in touch with me at the law office.'

He went on along the street and found the law office filled with Hank Belmont's crew. The town doctor was attending to Al Ensor and Jenny was crouching at the medical man's side. She looked up at Kendrick's entrance, shaking her head slowly in response to the unspoken question in his eyes. Kendrick sighed heavily, aware of what she was suffering. He went to her as she straightened to face him.

'The doctor isn't hopeful,' she reported harshly, 'but there is an outside chance. He's gonna be moved to the doctor's place shortly. Can I go along and stay with him?'

'Sure, and I'll arrange for a gun guard, in case the outlaws try to finish him off.' Kendrick shook his head. 'You know, we might have spared Al this trouble if you'd helped me when I first asked you.'

'I wish I had. But the situation wasn't clear then. I thought I could get Pa away from the gang with no trouble.'

Kendrick looked around the office. Pete Bardon was seated behind his desk, talking to Frank Belmont, and the half-dozen cowhands were talking excitedly about the action that was coming up.

'Frank, have two of your men go along when the doc moves Al Ensor out of here. I want him guarded at all times. You see to that.'

'You reckon someone might make another try for him?' The Circle B rancher came forward eagerly.

'It could happen. And get your men out of here. Have them get ready to ride out. I want the posse standing by. Have them take care of their horses.'

Belmont nodded and shouted at his crew. Two of them were detailed to guard the wounded pedlar. The others trooped out of the office. Kendrick went to Bardon.

'Lorimer has just ridden into town with half a dozen men, Pete. He's wetting his whistle in the saloon.'

'I'd better report to him.' Bardon got to his feet. 'Keep an eye on this place until I get back, huh?'

Kendrick nodded. He was filled with a growing impatience that made him restless. He needed to be out of town, closing in on the outlaws. He glanced at Jenny, crouching beside the doctor. How was he going to persuade her to leave Al long enough to show him the outlaw hideout? He saw the doctor lean towards her and speak in an undertone, and Jenny put her hands to her face and began weeping silently. Kendrick experienced a cold sensation in the pit of his stomach as the doctor got to his feet and came to him.

'Ensor's dead,' he said needlessly.

'I'm sorry, but there was little chance of saving him.'

'Thanks, Doc.' Kendrick stiffened his shoulders as the doctor departed. He went to Jenny's side and lifted her gently to her feet. She lowered her head to his broad shoulder and cried softly. He patted her shoulder. 'I'm sorry, Jenny,' he said. 'It's a bad business.'

She lifted her head and gazed up into his face. Her eyes were wet, over-bright, and filled with an ugly expression.

'Pa came to long enough to tell me that Trig Weevil shot him because the outlaws figured we'd both talked to you about the gang. He said Arch Kington and some of the rustlers are at the gang hideout, waiting for Darra to smash the local law so they can get back to their business. If you get your posse together I'll show you how to get into the hideout.'

'Right this minute?' Kendrick demanded.

'Get me a horse and we can hit the trail now,' she said remorselessly. 'If you want it that way, you can be facing

Darra and his bunch through gun-smoke when the sun comes up tomorrow morning.'

Kendrick nodded. 'You'd better stay with me,' he said. 'I don't want you to leave my side. Darra might have sent a man here to kill you. Come on, let's get some horses. I need to be riding out. I've had my fill of towns. I can't wait to hit the open trail and make for the hideout.' He paused and looked into her tearful face. 'Are you sure you know where the gang is?'

'I know.' She nodded, her expression fierce. 'I want to see the gang down in the dust for what they've done.'

Kendrick led the way to the street. One of Slater's cowhands was standing just outside the door, watching the street. Kendrick called to him.

'Stay inside the office until Pete Bardon, the deputy, returns,' he directed.

The cowhand nodded and Kendrick led Jenny along the street, calling to the few cowhands scattered along its length and telling them to report to Ben Slater. He found Slater in the saloon with the rest of his men, and the Bar S rancher was talking with Lorimer.

'Ben,' Kendrick said tersely, 'Belmont is getting his horses ready to travel. You'd better do the same. I'm riding out shortly. You've been trying to track down the rustlers who fired your spread. Well, I'm going out to their roost, and I guess you'll want to be in at the death, huh?'

'You can say that again!' Slater rapped. He finished his drink and turned to the batwings, calling to his men as he departed.

'I'll be at the stable in ten minutes,' Kendrick called after him. 'Tell Hank Belmont to be ready and waiting to ride.'

Slater departed, grinning in anticipation, and Kendrick looked into Lorimer's pale eyes and nodded.

'I got the information I need,' he told the sheriff, glancing at Jenny, who stood silently by his side.

'So she does know where the gang is located,' Lorimer said eagerly. 'We'd better take her into custody, where she'll be safe.'

'She's riding with me.' Kendrick's tone warned the sheriff that he would take no orders on the matter, or accept advice. 'Jenny knows a way into the hideout that will give us an advantage. We need her help if we're gonna finish off Darra and his bunch once for all.'

Lorimer nodded. 'It's in your hands,' he said tersely. 'Take that crooked bunch dead or alive, Chuck. I'll watch out for the law around here until you get back.'

Kendrick nodded and caught the tender's eye. He ordered a drink for Jenny and took a beer for himself. Jenny's face was ashen, her eyes filled with shock, and she rebelled when he insisted that she drink. But there was no fight in her now and she emptied her glass at a gulp when he kept on at her. He was pleased to see a trace of colour seep into her cheeks.

'See you when we get back, Abe,' Kendrick said by way of farewell, and took Jenny along to the stable.

The livery barn was a scene of bustle and activity. The Bar S and Circle B crews were preparing to travel. Horses were being watered, guns checked, and there was a sense of eagerness and anticipation among these men who had spent a week riding the range in a fruitless hunt for rustlers.

When they were ready to ride, Kendrick led his black out of the barn and swung into the saddle. Jenny mounted a chestnut and reined in beside him, and there was a clatter as the two outfits followed suit. The moon was up now, and shed pale light over the range as they left town. Jenny set a fast pace, but Kendrick had to curb his mount to remain at her side, his big stallion impatient to gallop. Slater and Belmont followed closely at the head of their men as they headed west.

Kendrick knew only a strong sense of satisfaction as they made their way towards the desert. For years he had dreamed of coming up against Darra and his gang for killing his father, and now he could hardly believe his luck that the outlaws seemed to be falling into his hands. He had no idea just how many bad men rode with Blink Darra, but he had more than a dozen hard-bitten cowpunchers at his back, and all were spoiling for a fight because of the losses suffered by their brands.

Jenny did not hesitate as she rode steadily through the night, and Kendrick felt sorry for the girl as he considered the situation. If she had helped him whole-heartedly back in Red Mesa her father would have survived, but reluctance had set her feet on a bitter trail, and he could imagine the line her thoughts were taking as they raised dust.

After two hours, Kendrick called a halt to rest their mounts, and the punchers dismounted and stood around in the close darkness, talking about the coming fight. Jenny moved off a few paces alone, and Kendrick joined her.

'How much further do we have to ride?' he asked.

'It's not far. We're close to the edge of the desert now, where Darra's horse ranch is. But we won't be able to ride straight in. The place is too well guarded for that. I know a back trail that will put us in a position overlooking the ranch yard, and it will be easy for you to sneak in and take the gang by surprise.'

'I doubt if it will be easy,' Kendrick rejoined. 'But all I ask is that you put us within sight of the place. I'll handle it from there.'

'You'll be looking down at Darra's roost come sunup,' she told him. 'But don't take any chances with them. They'll get away if you give them an inch. You need to kill them like the coyotes they are.'

They rode on, and false dawn was breaking when Jenny suddenly turned aside from the general direction they had taken from Singing Springs and began to ride across broken country. Kendrick wondered how many times she had been out here to the ranch, for she moved unerringly through the night. They rode through brush at a slower rate, and Kendrick suddenly realized that the faint trail was angling down a decline. He saw the walls of a gorge rising up on either side of them. Darkness closed in, and he felt stifled by the overhanging rocks hemming them in.

Presently the walls of the gorge widened and Jenny reined up. She slid tiredly from her saddle.

'This is as far as we go on horses,' she said. 'Now it's on foot. We climb that rock wall over there, and on the other side of it is the horse ranch.'

Kendrick relayed the information to the possemen, who ground-hobbled their mounts and took their rifles as they went on. Jenny followed a game trail that snaked through the rocks, and boots crunched on hard ground as they ascended the wall of the gorge. But they had covered only half the distance to the top when the trail reached a shelf, and they passed through a dark slit into a tunnel that was completely black.

'Hold on to each other.' Jenny's voice sounded just in front of Kendrick and he reached out and grasped her arm. Ben Slater's hand came out of the darkness from behind and took hold of Kendrick's belt. 'It's not far through here, and level.' Jenny's voice sounded ghostly in the blankness. 'Just keep hold of each other and come along. There's a tunnel just ahead, and then we'll be looking down on the ranch.'

They continued, and it seemed like an eternity to Kendrick. They were shuffling along blindly. His ears were strained to pick up surrounding noise but he heard nothing beyond the scuffing of boots on rock. Then Jenny halted, and the whole line of them paused. She struck a match and, to Kendrick's relief, lit a lantern standing on a small flat-topped rock. He looked around quickly, and saw that they were in a small cave.

'This is the back door to the hideout,' Jenny explained. 'It's a bolt-hole for use if the ranch is ever discovered by the law. Outside the cave, over there,' she pointed to the right, 'you can see the ranch. There'll be guards out — they're always on watch, and I should think dawn is breaking now. I've brought you this far. Now it's up to you. But be careful. There have been many attempts to capture this bunch but so far they've always managed to slip the law.'

'Their luck has just run out,' Kendrick said. 'Everyone stay in here while I take a look around outside. We need to take them by surprise, so no noise, huh?'

Jenny accompanied him and he left the cave, faintly surprised by the greying sky and the rosy glow on the eastern horizon heralding the advent of breaking day. He crouched in rocks and looked around, finding himself twenty feet above level ground. The buildings of a horse ranch were spread out below, showing indistinctly in the dim light of a new day. He studied the house and several smaller buildings, all made of adobe. There were three large corrals, two of them containing horses.

A man appeared from one of the smaller buildings and walked slowly across to the house. He was carrying a rifle, and paused in front of the house to subject his surroundings to an intent survey. Kendrick nodded. The outlaws were taking no chances, were serious about their security. He settled down to study the ranch, and saw another man squatting in cover, watching the approaches from the desert.

He saw that their only chance would be to surround the place and close in from all sides, and went back into the cave to acquaint the two cow outfits with the information.

'Then let's get to it,' Ben Slater said impatiently. 'Don't let's waste time. Those hellions could be planning to move out right now.'

They left the cave and Kendrick explained what he wanted them to do. Both Slater and Belmont agreed his plan, and the two ranchers led their crews off to surround the buildings. The sun was beginning to show its upper rim above the horizon, and Kendrick could almost feel the heat that was coming. He was unaccountably nervous, and realized that he was more afraid of losing the outlaws than fearing a clash with them.

Slater took his men to the right, stealing from cover to cover, intending to get into a position that would cut off the outlaws from their horses, and Belmont went to the left, intent on cutting off escape into the desert. Kendrick moved forward slowly with Jenny at his side. The girl was carrying a rifle and seemed determined to use it. He did not try to dissuade her.

When the possemen were in position in a rough circle, covering the ranch with their weapons, Kendrick moved forward in the growing daylight and hunkered down by a corner of the nearest corral. A man emerged from a cookshack, carrying two buckets, and made his way to a small creek. He filled the buckets and returned to the cookshack.

Looking around, Kendrick was about to shout a warning of their presence to the outlaws when he caught the faint drumming of hoofs approaching and rapidly growing louder. It sounded like many horses, and for a moment he was unable to pin-point the exact direction of their coming. Then he saw rising dust, and seven horses took shape as their riders pressed in from the desert and came riding boldly towards the ranch.

'They're some of the rustlers!' Jenny gasped. 'I can see Cal Pearson, and Arch Kington. They've been out on some mischief. What are you gonna do, Kendrick?'

The decision was taken from Kendrick. The rustlers must have spotted the posse, for the leaders suddenly shied away and started to flee. Before Kendrick could move, gunfire exploded raucously as the waiting possemen cut loose, and rustlers began to tumble out of their saddles. The horses milled as the tough cowhands fired rapidly, taking advantage of their surprise, and angered by their failure to locate the rustlers during the previous week.

Arch Kington fell heavily from his saddle and hit the ground hard. He did not move again. The rest of his men were swept from their saddles in short order, and Kendrick shook his head grimly as the last of them went down. He took no part in the shooting and quickly returned his attention to the ranch, for guns were firing from the buildings at the drifting gunsmoke marking the positions of the possemen. He clenched his teeth, fearing that the initiative had passed from him, and had a vision of the outlaws escaping from the net he had drawn around them.

'We're in a position to nail any of them who try to get away through the cave,' Jenny said. 'Darra won't stay and fight if he can run.'

Kendrick drew his pistol and cocked the weapon. He could see Hank Belmont running forward at the head of his men. They were making for the outlying buildings, vanishing into them and emerging again quickly, guns hammering and smoking. Kendrick wondered just how many outlaws were occupying the spread.

Jenny lifted her rifle and began shooting at the house, from which many puffs of gunsmoke drifted. Several men were emerging, running away from the building and completely disregarding the shooting. Ben Slater's outfit turned their guns on them, and Kendrick saw that the fleeing men were angling in his direction. He crouched beside Jenny and grasped her shoulder. She stopped shooting and turned an intent face towards him.

'Start shooting,' she rapped. 'You wanted Darra's bunch. Well, those men heading this way are it. That's Blink himself leading them, and I can see Weevil and Frayle with him. That trio will run while the rest of the bunch try to hold us off. That's how it always happens. Work your gun, Kendrick. This is what you came for.'

Kendrick gazed at the running outlaws, and recognized the face of Blink Darra from the wanted posters he had studied. A cold thrill tremored through him as he lifted his gun into the aim and began shooting, relishing the recoil of the big pistol as it bucked against the heel of his hand. He was taut inside, aware of the knowledge that at last he was facing the men responsible for his father's death. He had dreamed of this moment for years, and was hard-eyed, cold and purposeful. Gunsmoke flared from his gun muzzle, filling his nostrils with its sickening pungency and blowing into his eyes on the morning breeze. But nothing could detract from his determination and he worked his gun with cool deliberation.

Darra was coming straight at him, pistol in hand, a tall, heavily built man dressed in a dark store-suit. His coarse features were twisted into a snarl of defiance as he looked left and right, triggering his two pistols at fleeting targets until Kendrick's first shots reached him. Kendrick aimed for the man's belt buckle, but Darra changed direction as Kendrick's gun flamed and the bullet merely grazed his left hip. Kendrick shifted his aim and fired again. Darra stumbled, quickly caught his balance, and then went sprawling on the hard ground. He jumped up again, seemingly indestructible, his attention now fully upon Kendrick, and his big pistols blasted a string of shots.

Kendrick ducked low as slugs crackled around him, but did not stop triggering his gun. He felt the hot burn of a bullet across the top of his left shoulder. Another bored through the crown of his Stetson. A third nicked the lobe of his left ear. He returned fire, and saw Darra rear up to his knees, his guns falling from his big hands. Blood spurted from the outlaw's forehead as he slumped lifeless to the hard ground.

Kendrick was breathing shallowly through his mouth. He looked around. Jenny was firing into the mass of outlaws still coming towards them, and three of their number were already stretched out on the ground, testimony to the girl's accuracy and resolution. She was lying flat, the barrel of her rifle resting on a flat-topped rock, sending shot after shot into the running men. She had chosen her spot well, for she was lying in the path the outlaws had to take to get to their bolt-hole from the ranch.

Two of the outlaws were angling away from the others, and Kendrick was glad of the many hours he had spent studying the wanted posters of the Darra gang. He recognized Weevil and Frayle trying to sneak away and turned his deadly gun upon them. Weevil had killed Kendrick's father twelve years before, and now Kendrick concentrated on the outlaw, using the skills his father had taught him. He narrowed his eyes and fined down his senses to the running figure. Then he fired.

His first shot took Weevil in the left side as the man angled away. Weevil jumped but did not go down. He swung to face Kendrick at a distance of ten yards, lifting his pistol as if it had suddenly become too heavy to hold, his face twisted by desperate effort. The weapon flamed, and Weevil emptied it at the man who stood between him and escape. Kendrick ignored the lead that hammered around him. He aimed again at Trig Weevil's tall, thin figure and squeezed his trigger deliberately. His gun recoiled, and grim satisfaction thrilled through him when Weevil tumbled over backwards, his sixgun flying from suddenly nerveless fingers.

Ike Frayle was of medium build, inclined to obesity. His mouth was agape as he pounded along as fast as his short legs could carry him. His twin pistols blasted at the possemen behind him now rampaging through the ranch like a pack of hungry wolves. Kendrick lifted his smoking gun, and was surprised when it slipped out of his hand. He bent and scrabbled for it but his right arm was suddenly useless and there was blood pouring down his hand, making his fingers too slippery to grasp the weapon. There was no pain in his arm, which surprised him, and he was shocked by the quantity of blood escaping from him.

Frayle was facing him now, shifting his aim towards Kendrick, who dropped to one knee and reached for his gun with his left hand.

'Jenny,' he called urgently, aware that he was not going to make it. Frayle was already triggering his guns, and Kendrick dropped flat to avoid the hail of lead that crackled around him.

Jenny had emptied her rifle at the running outlaws and was resorting to the pistol she had buckled around her waist. She glanced at Kendrick, saw his predicament, and swung her sixgun to cover Frayle. The outlaw, thinking that he had accounted for Kendrick, was turning away again, angling left with just one thought in his mind — escape.

'Frayle!' Jenny yelled in a shrill voice. 'Hold it right there. You're not going anywhere. It's pay-off time.'

The outlaw heard her call and turned his head quickly, pausing in surprise when he recognized her.

'For my father!' Jenny called, and triggered her gun at Frayle until the hammer clicked on an empty cartridge.

Four chunks of hot lead struck Frayle. He toppled over backwards and lay unmoving. Kendrick stared at the inert body, seeing in his mind's eye his father shooting it out with the outlaws until they put him down in the dust. A bitter sigh escaped him and he made an effort to break the sense of inertia gripping him. As he looked around the ranch the pain of the wound in his right shoulder hit him. He sagged to the ground, clenching his teeth. He pressed his left hand against the gory hole in his shoulder and squeezed hard, but could not stop the flowing blood. Then the ground seemed to spring up at him. His forehead hit a rock and he blacked out.

When he regained his senses he was lying on the hard ground with the sun shining in his eyes. Sweat was pouring from him and pain racked his body. A terrible thirst was searing his insides. He lifted his head and looked around, seeking his hat, troubled by the glaring sun. There was deep silence, and he saw armed men wandering around the ranch, which alarmed him until he recognized them as possemen. The reek of dissipating gunsmoke clung to his nostrils. His hat was lying on the ground beside him and he reached for it with his right hand. But the movement released all the torments of hell in his shoulder and he relaxed instantly.

'Don't move or you'll bust open your wound, and I had a big job stanching the flow of blood.' Jenny appeared in his line of vision and dropped to her knees at his side. She was holding a canteen and lifted his head gently, dribbling some water into his parched mouth. Her eyes were hard, her expression showing shock and grief, but she smiled encouragingly at him. 'You're gonna be all right,' she told him. 'The shoulder will heal. I don't know if you'll ever be as good with a gun again as you were.'

'What about the gang?' he demanded, using his left hand to tip the canteen to increase the flow of water into his parched mouth.

'All done.' She smiled then and her eyes glinted. 'You got your wish. Ben Slater is gonna bring a buckboard over here to pick you up. We got several men wounded, and the sooner we get you all back to Singing Springs the better. Now lie quiet and rest up.'

'Sure. Just drop my hat over my eyes, huh?'

She did so, and Kendrick closed his eyes. His mind seemed curiously empty, and he realized that the nagging urge to avenge his father's death had finally left him. There was now a comforting void where it had festered, and he felt as if he had been reborn. He relaxed, and found pleasure in not having to concentrate on law work. The knowledge that it was done and finished with filled him with relief. But a sudden prickling sensation in the back of his mind disturbed him and he opened his eyes.

'Jenny,' he called urgently.

'I'm here,' she said softly. 'I'm not going anywhere. My pa is dead and now I've got no one. You've been sticking your nose into my life lately, and I realize now that you were trying to help me, so I'll be around to take care of you until you get back on your feet.'

'We'll work something out,' he promised, and had a feeling that she would be around for the rest of his life.

We do hope that you have enjoyed reading this large print book.

Did you know that all of our titles are available for purchase?

We publish a wide range of high quality large print books including:
Romances, Mysteries, Classics
General Fiction
Non Fiction and Westerns

Special interest titles available in large print are:
The Little Oxford Dictionary
Music Book, Song Book
Hymn Book, Service Book

Also available from us courtesy of Oxford University Press:
Young Readers' Dictionary
(large print edition)
Young Readers' Thesaurus
(large print edition)

For further information or a free brochure, please contact us at:
Ulverscroft Large Print Books Ltd.,
The Green, Bradgate Road, Anstey,
Leicester, LE7 7FU, England.
Tel: (00 44) **0116 236 4325**
Fax: (00 44) **0116 234 0205**

A TOWN CALLED
TROUBLESOME

John Dyson

Matt Matthews had carved his ranch out of the wild Wyoming frontier. But he had his troubles. The big blow of '86 was catastrophic, with dead beeves littering the plains, and the oncoming winter presaged worse. On top of this, a gang of desperadoes had moved into the Snake River valley, killing, raping and rustling. All Matt can do is to take on the killers single-handed. But will he escape the hail of lead?

BRAZOS STATION

Clayton Nash

Caleb Brett liked his job as deputy sheriff and being betrothed to the sheriff's daughter, Rose. What he didn't like was the thought of the sheriff moving in with them once they were married. But capturing the infamous outlaw Gil Bannerman offered a way out because there was plenty of reward money. Then came Brett's big mistake — he lost Bannerman and was framed. Now everything he treasured was lost. Did he have a chance in hell of fighting his way back?